LITTLE BLACK TRAINS

Bob Chaundy

A tale of life, death and commuting

Shaftoe Publishing

First published in 2013 by Shaftoe Publishing

http://www.littleblacktrains.com

ISBN 978-0-9576674-1-9

To rail commuters everywhere, and to all obituary writers who bring to life the unique stories of the newly departed.

There's a little black train a-comin'

Comin' down the track;

You gotta ride that little black train,

But it ain't a gonna bring you back.

Woody Guthrie

CONTENTS

She slid her key hurriedly into the lock, twisted it and pushed the door that opened into her well-lit hallway. In a series of movements that resembled a rehearsed stage routine, she threw her handbag on to the wooden chair, removed her jacket and flung it over the banister with her left arm while at the same time kicking the door shut with her right heel. Festooned along the length of the hall were photographs of her, several with microphone in hand, against the backdrop of exotic foreign locations. There she stood upon the old bridge at Mostar in Herzegovina, beneath the Victory Arch in Baghdad, surrounded by smiling troops at Camp Bastion in Afghanistan. She checked her hair in the reflection from one of the glass frames that confirmed how much greyer it had become since the photo was taken. She moved into the kitchen where she immediately opened the refrigerator and grabbed the sandwich that she'd forgotten to take with her that day for which her stomach had been punishing her for the past hour. She was never to eat it. Before she turned round, a bullet fired from behind her at point-blank range exploded into her head splattering fragments of hair, skull and brain on to the fridge door. In the midst of the bloody mess was a magnet that read, *Sometimes I wake up grumpy, other days I let him sleep.*

1 CHAIN REACTION

"They call us names, ladies and gentlemen, like Doctor Death or the Grim Reaper. We work the Death Beat. People constantly ask us who will be the next to die as if we obituarists somehow are privy to the workings of fate. If only. A colleague once said of me that when Ben Murray asks how you are, it's a loaded question." Better pause there, might even get a laugh, thought Ben as he manoeuvred his bicycle past a rat lying in the gutter. "Strange place to sunbathe", he mused.

There was something preternatural about the day, a vague sense that things wouldn't follow their normal course. It wasn't just that reciting aloud in the street could result in being sectioned, but that the stilted tenor of the delivery required to an audience rather than to the traffic lights, roundabout and T-junction was somewhat embarrassing to one with a far from extravagant nature. Then there was the rumble of thunder. Thunder in the morning? Unheard of. A premonition of trouble ahead perhaps? Ah, someone rolling out a wheelie bin.

Ben had delivered this presentation on the art of the obituary so many times he knew it off by heart, well almost, hence the rehearsal. He'd given the speech to national and international media conferences where the organisers had sought a variety of different topics and viewed obituaries as a quirky alternative to the more predictable items on the agenda. To Ben, the lecture was a labour of love, encapsulating all the reasons why he had revelled in the job of Obituaries Editor at BBC News for 15 years. Obituaries represented diversity. Each life was unique, each subject had excelled at something even if it was just sticking two fingers up at authority. On the other hand, crime figures, A-Level results, hospital waiting-lists, budgets, Queen's speeches, party conferences and all the other news subjects with which his colleagues were involved came round each year, every year and barely differed in their treatment. Ben found many of his subjects inspiring even if the word "obituaries" had a deathly ring to those outside the Fourth Estate and to some within it. Whenever Ben was asked at a social gathering what kind of work he did, his answer invariably raised a smile. So he tended just to describe himself as a journalist and only advertise his specialism if the questioner dug deeper. If they did, they were invariably both interested and interesting. He'd read about a well-known Australian obituary writer, Mark McGinness, who once attended a party with Dame Maggie Smith. She asked him what he did for a living and when he told her, he was subjected to "an icy stare of utter disdain". As McGinness recalled, "No one does disdain quite like Dame Maggie Smith."

Mostly, Ben had presented his lecture to young journalist students, though they did not always share his enthusiasm for the lives of "old people", at least not until he had finished speaking. The members of the Hammersmith branch of the Women's Institute whom he was addressing this morning were more likely to appreciate his line of work. After all, they'd invited him, he hadn't offered. And they would be older too, and what's more, there'd be cakes.

"Any notion that compiling obituaries is a macabre pursuit, ladies and gentlemen," Ben continued, as a grinding noise emanated from his 30-year-old Raleigh Pathfinder, "should be dispelled immediately. For obits are about life, not death. Not so the slap and clammy slither of the circumscribing clay for the obit writer. Yes, we may apply a touch of verbal rouge here and literary mascara there in the manner of media undertakers anxious to show off our craft in a good light. But death is the mere pretext for our work; the gory details belong in the news pages or, in the case of broadcast obits, in the presenter's introduction. Instead obituaries, whether broadcast or in print, celebrate a life lived in all its richness, charting the successes, the failures, the tragedies, the hilarious, the heroism, the daring, the fame, the infamy." He was becoming so carried away with his own eloquence that Ben nearly crashed into a parked car. There was another grinding noise from his bike. Ben gave a casual glance at the source of the noise, ignored it and carried on.

"What could be macabre about having to listen to Gielgud in his prime soliloquising Shakespeare in a voice 'all cello and woodwind'? What can be more uplifting than seeing Gregory Peck sermonising in court so eloquently against racism in the deep south of America, or hearing Zsa Zsa Gabor when asked how many husbands she had, say 'What, of my own?'"

He rode onto the pavement to avoid a one-way street, scattering in his wake a flock of pigeons pecking on scraps of bread thrown out by the owner of a bakery shop as he prepared to open on a brand new morning.

"What's gory about reliving the elegance of Fred Astaire, the aristocrat of dance, and Gene Kelly, his proletarian equivalent, or the oratory of Sir Winston Churchill, or Martin Luther King? And what can be more creatively indulgent for the obituary writer than delving into the extraordinary lives of entertainers, scientists, artists, clerics, miscreants, and eccentrics. People such as Sir Hugh Rankin who, as summed up in The Daily Telegraph, was variously a riveter's mate, a trooper in the cavalry, a sheep-shearer in Australia, president of the British Muslim Society, vice-president of the World's Buddhist Association, a Welsh Republican Nationalist and a campaigner for 'an independent Red Republic of all Scotland, excluding the Orkneys and Shetland.' You couldn't make it up, ladies and gentlemen."

Ladies and gentlemen? Of course, only ladies will be present. As he waited at traffic lights, a fellow cyclist wearing a multi-coloured helmet and hunched over a gleaming racing bike, flashed past him, completely ignoring the red light. Ben scowled in disapproval before mounting the pavement again to take a short cut. The irony did not escape him. Another grinding noise. Ignore it.

"Obituaries can breathe life into a dead subject, at least in literal terms, ladies (no, that sounds patronising, better drop 'ladies'.) Not only can they remind you of people you'd long forgotten about and probably thought had died years ago, they can also illuminate aspects of lives of which you had no inkling. Take the actress Hedy Lamarr, star of such films as White Cargo and Samson and Delilah. She also found time to invent an early form of spread spectrum communications technology, which if you didn't know (pause again for possible laughter) is a key to modern wireless communication and designed to jam the guiding systems on enemy torpedoes. I kid you not, ladies...I kid you not. And there's the haematologist Dr John Wilkinson who not only trained sea lions to defuse bombs in World War II, a bizarre enough activity in itself, but also found time to amass a famous collection of apothecary jars, to be awarded the Silver Wolf, the Boy Scouts movement's highest honour, to help discover the cure for pernicious anaemia and to invent an early version of the zip fastener. How does that make you feel about your own life, ladies?" Damn, said it again.

Ben twisted his wrist to free his watch that had partially caught under his sleeve. It revealed that he was in good time being only five minutes from the station, which is to say he'd arrive five minutes before the train was due. He knew only too well the time margins within which he needed to operate in order to arrive on time. If only the trains were as reliable as their passengers was a constant thought. Ben was never one to be lured by the trappings of postmodernist status inherent in the automobile. Moving from A to B was simply a matter of practicality and travelling by bike 15 minutes each way every weekday saved the planet, avoided traffic jams and was free from the exorbitant car-park charges. What's more, it kept him fit, an important consideration for a man just turned 50 and vulnerable to taunts from his wife Elizabeth about his encroaching middle-age spread. He had little need to factor the vagaries of traffic flows into his timing equation, which made life even easier. Except, that is, when his bicycle chain comes off.

"Oh no, please not now of all days," he moaned, suddenly not caring if anyone heard him. He should have seen it coming since the chain had started to slip several days earlier. But he would rather ignore a mechanical problem than accept it existed. He had given up on buying a half-decent bike after having three stolen in the past. The last one had vanished a few days before Christmas no doubt he thought to be polished up and to appear under the tree with a red ribbon tied onto the handlebars.

By the time he had eventually succeeded in restoring it to bicycle, his temper was as filthy as his hands and the chances of making the train he reckoned to be only 50-50 provided, of course, that it didn't slip off again. It didn't, despite much furious pedalling and an internal argument as to whether or not all the effort was worth it. It was going to be touch and go. On arrival at the station, he didn't even bother locking his bike, not only for reasons of time but also because, in his mood, he'd have been quite happy for a thief to help himself. He dashed up the steps into the main concourse, plunged his oil-stained fingers into his back pocket for his season ticket, fed it into the barrier, and, as he pulled it out again, saw his train moving off from the platform. Instinctively, out of sheer frustration, Ben aimed a fly-kick at the ticket rugby-style. What was supposed to be a minor act of juvenile petulance turned into something rather more significant. His slip-on shoe, rather like his bicycle chain, had been growing looser over the past few weeks. It shot off his foot high into the air in a spiralling motion, cracked loudly against a windowpane and lodged, spectacularly, on to a steel rafter. The station went quiet as Ben, numb with embarrassment, was caught in a crossfire of disbelieving stares. This was indeed an unusual day and this was only the start.

"What the hell did you think you were doing?"

As if things weren't bad enough, the shout came from Ben's least favourite ticket inspector, a squat man in his early fifties dressed in his dark grey railwayman's uniform and a face flushed with anger. A few weeks ago, Ben had had a run-in with him after he'd been caught trying to board a train using an off-peak ticket when it was still officially peak time. No manner of polite argument that the train was late and had entered the off-peak period and his persistent mention of the number of times he'd had to stand all the way to London, had held sway. The inspector was unimpressed by Ben's dubious reinterpretation of the rules and had practically frog-marched him back to the ticket hall in full public view. Now, though, the indignity was self-imposed.

"I was kicking my ticket," came the pathetic reply.

"Kicking your ticket?"

"Yes, I was, um, I was, I'd missed my train and..."

"Kicking your ticket?"

"Yes, I was fed up so I...

"Kicking your ticket?"

"Yes, you heard," Ben retorted angrily.

He couldn't help himself. He knew he was in no position to be anything but meek, but this megalomaniac rubbed him up the wrong way.

"Don't take that tone of voice with me, mate. Besides, you could have broken a bloody window."

The two men stood only a couple of metres apart, close enough for Ben to feel the anger that surged from the inspector's piercing stare. Ben raised his hands in submission. Even though he bridled at the word "mate", given the circumstances, he offered, "You're right, I'm sorry, I was stupid. I let my temper get the better of me."

"I should bloody well think so," came the reply. "We have enough trouble with teenage hooligans let alone middle-aged ones."

Ben let that remark pass. He became yet more submissive.

"Um, there's one thing, though. I need my shoe. I need to get it down."

"Oh yeah?"

This was excruciating for Ben. Humiliation heaped upon humiliation. Bad enough apologising, now he needed help.

"Do you have a ladder or something?"

"What do you mean by something?"

Ben had no idea what he meant by "something". It was just "something" he said.

"Shall I call for superman or what's his name, the human fly?"

Suddenly, the ticket inspector was starting to enjoy himself, displaying reserves of rapier wit hitherto not countenanced by those whose tickets he inspected daily. His face had reverted back to its normal grey pallor.

"Shall I ring Chris Bonington?"

"Seriously, do you have a ladder?"

"Oh dear, I've forgotten to bring mine with me today." The inspector was by now playing to a gallery of assembled bystanders anxious to know exactly what had happened. If Ben's face showed a resentful resignation to this sarcastic onslaught, it was to transform in an instant to one of gratitude when the Polish girl serving in the coffee kiosk kindly informed him that some window cleaners were working round the corner. After the embarrassment of explaining himself to the pair of bemused workmen, he requisitioned the ladder and holding it upright made the brief, if slightly lopsided walk towards the wall at the top of which rested his shoe.

"I'm not sure we can allow this," shouted the inspector, his redness reappearing. "There are health and safety issues to be considered."

Ben was about to swear but held himself in check. "I'll go up at my own risk and if I fall down you'll have the pleasure of sweeping up my remains."

The inspector smiled at the very thought. Then Ben's visage took on a nervous demeanour. No, it was not a fear of heights; he realised that his commuter pals were starting to arrive for the train he would normally have caught at 8.25.

"What the fuck?" uttered a bemused Steve Graham on seeing his one-shoed friend crabbing his way across the ticket hall, ladder in hands.

"Don't ask," said Ben.

"What the fuck are you doing?"

"Retrieving my shoe."

"He was kicking his ticket," shouted the inspector, once again beaming with delight.

"And his shoe came off."

"Kicking his ticket?"

By now, Robbie Blake had arrived. "What's going on?" he asked Steve.

"Apparently, he was kicking his ticket and his shoe came off."

"Kicking his ticket?" The two began laughing as Ben began ascending the ladder.

"You'd better hop on the next train, mate," cackled Steve.

"Love your sock," added Robbie.

The frivolity became infectious and even people who didn't know Ben personally were smirking at his expense. Steve Graham suggested that if he ever wrote Ben's obituary, he'd include this anecdote in it, one that illuminated in a telling and humorous way a certain aspect of his personality. Before Ben could ask him of what aspect of his personality he was thinking, he lost him in the commuter scrum.

After the usual pushing and shoving that accompanies boarding a train in rush hour, Ben eventually found a seat opposite his friend Hilary, a pretty fair-haired thirtysomething recently returned to work as a solicitor a year after the birth of her first child. Having witnessed the end of the fracas in the ticket hall, she was still smirking. Itching to immerse herself in the thriller she was reading, she allowed herself a single comment.

"Thank God it was you and not Steve arguing with that inspector. I think Steve would have rammed his other shoe down the man's throat."

Ben nodded. Next to them, occupying the two window seats, sat two grey-suited men also in their thirties whom Ben determined within seconds were two IT consultants. Ben would normally chat to a friend or read the paper but he was still winding down from his morning rigours and Hilary was engrossed in her book. So he listened in on a conversation that turned out to be so impenetrable to ordinary mortals, the pair might have been speaking in tongues. He almost felt sorry for one. He seemed to be having trouble configuring his control protocols, and to make matters worse, his snap-ins had failed to initialise. When the IT men got off at the next station, Ben turned to Hilary.

"Did you understand a single word those guys were saying?"

"Maybe it was a secret code, Ben," Hilary replied shooting him a momentary glance. "Maybe one was telling the other where Lord Lucan is and you've missed a scoop. Serves you right for listening, you're a typical journalist, a nosy parker."

"I'm not a nosy parker, I have an enquiring mind."

Hilary smiled ruefully.

"Anyway, I didn't want to listen but they spoke so loudly I couldn't avoid it. It's not as if I joined in. Couldn't even if I'd wanted to."

"Do you often join in private conversations?" Hilary enquired, still not raising her eyes from her book.

"Not often, I am a southerner after all. Mind you, I did the other day. I heard these two agonising over who played the leading man in Brief

Encounter. I let it go for as long as I could and then had to tell them it was Alec Guinness."

As he spoke, what looked like a mother and daughter, around 60 and 40 years respectively, asked to be let in to the window seats previously occupied by the IT men. The mother was expensively dressed in a beige suit and wore a pearl necklace while her daughter was more casual in jeans and houndstooth check jacket. Ben and Hilary stood up to let them squeeze past. As soon as they had sat down, the mother said in hushed tones yet just loud enough for their two neighbours to hear, "Darling, I'm going to tell you something now that's going to shake you." At this, Ben made a wide-eyed expression of anticipation to Hilary who responded with a raised eyebrow. He grabbed one of the free newspapers scattered around the carriage and pretended to read it. The mother proceeded to confess to her daughter that her first son, the daughter's elder brother, was in fact the result of an affair she'd enjoyed with an American serviceman at the beginning of the Second World War. There followed a detailed explanation not only of the circumstances surrounding this illicit relationship but the reasons why she was admitting to it after so many years. The daughter was reduced to moist-eyed, open-mouthed shock and bewilderment and only occasionally interrupted her mother's flow for the purposes of clarification. Ben was busily re-reading the same line. As the explanation for the revelations began to unfold, a series of inane tannoy announcements made it impossible for Ben to decipher what the mother and daughter were saying. There were so many questions Ben wanted answering. He hadn't quite caught if the son/brother of this mother and daughter had ever been told the truth about his parentage. He wondered if the GI had ever been told that he had a son. Did the husband know the child wasn't his? And what effect had all this had had on the marriage?

"Why didn't you ask her, nosy parker?" said Hilary facetiously after he'd shared his thoughts with her once the women had disembarked. "Steve probably would have," she added.

"Yes, and Steve would have been deservedly slapped in the face. Come on, Hilary, you're not trying to tell me you weren't earwigging like mad."

"I was a little distracted perhaps," she admitted, smilingly, in her customary understated manner.

"A little distracted? You were barely pretending to read your book any more than I was this paper."

Hilary smiled again, looked at Ben and said, "I must confess I thought the daughter was going to faint at one point when she told her about the brother's real Dad."

Ben erupted in laughter.

"And by the way," she added, "It was Trevor Howard not Alec Guinness."

"Who, the father?"

"No, idiot, the leading man in Brief Encounter."

"Yes, yes, I knew that, I was testing you. I wanted to know whether you would you have told them it was Trevor Howard?"

"Maybe."

"I thought so. We're all nosy parkers, Hilary, even you."

"Not at all," she murmured, packing her book into her bag. "Just my enquiring mind."

2 CARLA

On his arrival back at London's Television Centre, Ben opened the door of the BBC News obituaries office on which were attached two quotations. One from Jimi Hendrix read, "Once you're dead, you're made for life", the other by an obituary writer called Andrew Losowsky that announced "We give good dead." As Ben entered the room, Keith Boswell, a grey-haired and bearded man in his late fifties and who looked after radio obits, let forth an anguished cry. Ben knew straight away what was behind it. Keith had just driven into the water on the 17th at Sawgrass thus ruining what had been up to then a highly promising round. Keith and Ben were deadly rivals at computer golf. They were consistently vying with each other in any spare minutes as to who would hold the office record. Each time it was shattered, either one would make an almost ritual run around the room beaming with competitive zeal and high-fiving everyone in a virtual gallery. Once, when Ben had phoned in to inform his team that he'd suffered a couple of cracked ribs in a minor car crash, Keith, after showing cursory sympathy, couldn't wait to inform him that a far more important breakage was Ben's long-held office record of 65. It set Ben's recovery back at least a day.

Ben looked across to his other colleague, Anthony Dukes who was so used to the howls of disappointment emanating from the other side of the room that it barely registered. Anyway, he was too busy tinkering with a script on his computer while gently singing to himself Bob Dylan songs in the voice of Noel Coward. It had become his speciality to write an insightful, crafted obituary on a philosopher, novelist or whomsoever while intoning in clipped English.

"Come gather rind people wherever you roam."

Next to Ben's desk hung a toy monkey with a button that when pressed set off a series of simian shrieks. It owed its presence to a play on words. A work experience intern had accused Anthony one day of being a romantic manqué. The next day the accuser appeared with her "romantic monkey". The idea struck Ben after the joke had worn off, that the monkey could be the office's equivalent of the Lutine Bell. At Lloyd's of London, this bell would be rung whenever a ship was lost at sea. Now, it's also rung to denote the death of a member of the Royal Family or major disasters such as 9/11. Whenever the news came through of a death for which an obituary had been prepared, the cry went out to "spank the monkey".

The intern was known as The Stick. In her mid-twenties, six foot tall and skinny enough to hide behind a rake, she had knocked on the door of the office unannounced one day and asked if she could join the team voluntarily to write obits. Anthony had inquired as to why on earth a young woman such as her would want to do such a thing. She answered that she held a fascination for celebrity death, had a passion for writing about people's lives and wanted to learn from the best. The flattery secured her a trial since she was asking for no money, was keen and, it transpired, possessed a gossamer touch of a writing style so suited to the broadcast medium. Against that, she was as emotionally fragile as a pane of sugar glass and her tales of unrequited love and fractured relationships kept Ben and his colleagues entertained behind her back. In her lean-limbed way Ben found her quite beautiful. Tall, blond and with swimming pool blue eyes, she was in Anthony's ironic phrase, "the epitome of Aryan womanhood". Yet her porcelain complexion only emphasised the vulnerability engendered in her slender frame. She was thin but not emaciated and despite the troubles in her private life that she attracted like bees to honey, she bore a steely determination that Ben was convinced would serve her well in her future career. After all, why else, he wondered, would a young girl want to share an office and a workload with three middle-aged men? These men had difficulty remembering her real name, Mairede, let alone spell it, so the name The Stick stuck.

Ben was in mind of a New York Times journalist, Russell Baker who once asserted that obituaries serve as "oases of calm in a world gone mad".

Compared to the newsroom's often-joyless grind of producing TV and radio packages at high speed to tight deadlines, the obituaries department was to Ben an oasis of insanity within BBC News. However, he had to insist to colleagues that persistent rumours that a cheer could be heard in the corridor outside the obits office on the announcement of a major death were, to borrow an obit phrase, an exaggeration.

"How did you get on with the ladies?" asked Anthony, interrupting his "I'm afraid I'm unable to work on Margaret's farm any longer" routine.

"It was going fine, nobody fell asleep, they laughed in all the right places, gave me plenty of applause when I'd finished, but then it came to the questions."

"Oh yeah, give you a hard time, did they?"

"You aren't kidding. I was expecting the usual stuff about what were my favourite obits, who's the most famous person you've ever met, have I ever killed someone off before they'd died and all that, but no. The very first question I get is from some formidable looking old blue rinse who gets up, points at me and says, 'How come women don't get as many obituaries as men?' She then starts quoting research done in America and Australia that shows that men outnumber women in obits four to one. 'And I'm sure the same goes for our country,' she says, 'so what's your answer to that?'

"And what was it, pray?" asked Anthony with a glint in his eye.

Ben explained how he told his audience that in his opinion obituaries simply reflected society. The majority of obituaries are people who were in their prime in the 1940s and '50s when few women were able to forge high-flying careers. As he pointed out, nowadays girls sail single-handedly round the world in their teens. The questioner didn't seem entirely satisfied and suggested that the poor ratio might have something to do with her estimation that nearly all obituary editors were male. Suddenly Ben found himself being cast as representing the epitome of male bias in modern society. There followed an animated discussion about the criteria for choosing an obit subject.

“While I have nothing against men fighting battles or crossing the Arctic or whatever if they’re stupid enough to want to do that,” continued the lady in question to a few gasps, and one or two chuckles from around the hall. “But what’s wrong with feminine qualities? How about the widow who, for the sake of argument, brought up two kids on her own on a council estate and then spent years manning the phones of the Samaritans helping the suicidal. Why can’t she have an obit instead of these boring male civil servants who had it easy all their working lives, got given a CBE for time-serving and a fat index-linked pension when they retired?”

“Right on, Doris,” shouted someone from the back to much amusement.

“If she’d founded the Samaritans, she might make an obit,“ said Ben cheekily.

“I suppose a man did that,” replied the woman.

“Afraid so.”

Ben related how relieved he was that the meeting ran out of time and he rounded it off diplomatically by saying that two of the domains popular for obituaries in which women rarely feature are infamy and heroic failure. He also added that broadcast obituaries, because of the nature of the media they serve, were almost always famous people and that the male to female ratio was far more balanced than in the print media.

“Are you sure about that?” said Keith.

“No.”

“Well I’ve just done a count for the last year while you were talking.”

“Go on, give it to me.”

"80/20 in favour of men."

"Oops".

"So how are we going to even up the ratio?" asked The Stick looking decidedly disgruntled.

Ben shrugged his shoulders.

"Short of hiring a hit-man to mow down the casts of *Desperate Housewives* and *Sex in the City*, in the short-term there ain't nothing we can do."

"And in the long-term? The Stick asked again, wide-eyed with expectancy.

"That's why I hired you," he answered, smiling at the lameness of his reply.

Ben explained to The Stick that when he first assumed the responsibilities of the BBC's news obituaries, he saw it as a challenge since the department was in a state of neglect. This was because the duties were shared by newsroom journalists on a haphazard, rotational basis usually by people either drying out or who had insulted the Director-General's wife at an official function, or both.

"There'd have been questions in parliament if we hadn't had something decent to run if one of the royals had snuffed it," he remembered his news editor saying at the time. "Imagine what fun the right-wing press would have had." So, a dedicated team that could devote itself entirely to the tender loving care of rectifying this state of affairs was born. Prime ministers, presidents, religious leaders and royals were among the categories of subjects decreed to be de rigeur to have a pre-prepared obituary ready and waiting for broadcast.

Ben's stock had risen immeasurably when Princess Diana was killed. He was on holiday in Spain on that August day when her car crashed in Paris. An irritating neighbour woke him up by banging on his door early on the Sunday morning, shouting, "Did you do her obituary?" "Did I do whose obituary?" came the reply in an "I drunk too much Rioja last night so why are you waking me up at this ungodly hour" manner. The initial shock and incredulity on being told of Diana's death was soon replaced by a surge of adrenalin when Ben remembered having updated the obituary only a few weeks before. He immediately turned on the TV and, lo and behold, caught the end of his obit. "YES, YES," Ben exclaimed leaping in the air as if he'd just sunk a hole-in-one, or scored the winning goal in the Cup Final. His neighbour, still reeling under the shock of Diana's death, looked on in dismay and bewilderment. Ben lived with the strange paradox that there was a part of him that wanted people to die. This apparent cruelty, as he was constantly pointing out, was only a professional desire, give or take the odd member of a rival football team. But having diligently prepared an obit often over several days, it was natural for obituarists such as he to want to see the fruits of his or her work published or broadcast. Ben called base to check if everything was in order with the obituary. He was told that the presenter in particular liked it because at around 10 minutes long he had to time for a toilet break. Praise indeed!

Ben walked over to the coat stand where he carefully hung his jacket. His desk lay between Anthony's and The Stick's on one side of the room while Keith occupied the other next to a host of radio equipment including a reel-to-reel tape player and a CD unit. Ben was about to turn his computer on when his phone rang.

"Hello, morgue here."

The smile on Ben's face was extinguished by the words of the caller.

"What?"

Ben felt a tremble as adrenaline gushed into his veins. Then after a pause, "I don't believe it."

Another pause. "What happened?"

As he waited for his caller's answer, Keith's phone rang. Anthony and The Stick looked with concern and bemusement at Ben. When he put the phone down a few seconds later, Keith was uttering into his phone similar expressions to those Ben had just mouthed.

"Well?" asked Anthony as Ben cast an incredulous look in their direction.

"Carla Wilson has been murdered - shot dead."

"You're kidding," exclaimed Anthony in disbelief. The Stick put her hands to her mouth, her eyes moistening. By now, Keith who had received the same news sped into their side of the room, visibly shaking.

"I used to work with her when she was a lowly sub in the newsroom, long before she became the hot-shot foreign correspondent. She was lovely. Who would want to kill her?"

Ben shrugged his shoulders and fired up his computer and assumed an air of authority. "Anthony, you look after the website, I'll do the telly, Stick you shadow me."

Ben's phone rang again, and again and again. Office tinnitus he called it. Correspondents, news bulletin editors, 24-hour news editors, website editors, picture librarians, edit suite controllers, news producers even subtitlers were all wanting to speak with him. Ben had to commandeer The Stick to field the calls. As he made his way at almost running pace to the newsroom, he recalled how much simpler life had been before 24-hour news and the internet had existed. As he entered he saw a flock of people of all designations gathered around the bulletin editor's desk, some in tears at the shock of losing a colleague.

The newsroom meeting lasted less than five minutes as far as Ben's participation was concerned since the programme editor was understandably more taken with the on-the-spot news angle and a discussion with the Channel Controller about organising a news flash. However, it was self-evident that what was required was an assortment of Carla's most memorable assignments both abroad – in the wars in Iraq, Afghanistan and Bosnia - as well as more recently at home as the crime correspondent. The editor also mentioned a famous clip of her tap-dancing with Bruce Forsyth though no one could quite remember whether it was on Children in Need or Comic Relief. The Head of News had already called to offer a tribute soundbite for the obit and the editor agreed that in the circumstances Ben could have around five minutes but that he need not worry about the exact duration given that most of the bulletin would be devoted to the subject. Ben then returned to his office where Anthony and Keith were both typing away furiously.

"I love the smell of adrenaline in the morning," said Anthony looking like the cat who got the cream.

"You're licking your lips you cynical old hack. Any of you know which programme Carla Wilson was dancing with Bruce Forsyth on?"

"Nope," said Keith shrugging his shoulders.

"Antiques Roadshow?" suggested Anthony.

Ben arranged for reams of pictures from a cross-section of Carla's programmes to be fed into the central server. Above all, he wanted a clip of Carla herself saying something interesting about her work or her life, something universal. This was something he would normally try to find himself but given the urgency, he had to leave it to a librarian. Ben derived great satisfaction from finding the perfect sound bite that best encapsulated the essence of his subject. He had many favourites: Bernard Manning justifying his opinion that immigrants aren't really English with "Just because a dog is born in a stable doesn't mean it's a horse." There was Victor Borge, the humorist and concert pianist, known as the Clown Prince of Denmark, saying, "I learnt to play on my mother's knee; we couldn't afford a piano." Or Margaret Thatcher's tribute to her deputy Willie Whitelaw, "Every Prime Minister needs a Willie." Or Willie Whitelaw himself, accusing Harold Wilson of "going round the country stirring up apathy".

As Ben hurried with The Stick towards the edit suite, he recalled to her how, when he first trained to be a broadcast journalist, his instructor told him something that always stuck in his mind, namely always try to come up with a good beginning and a good ending. "If you do so," he told The Stick, "the middle won't matter." Thus, an actor's obit would always open with one of the subject's most dramatic scenes, or a singer's would start with a best-known song, or a politician's with a rousing speech. The American comedian George Burns unwittingly provided his own with the line, "When I get up in the morning the first thing I do is open my newspaper and look at the obituary column. If I'm not in it I have breakfast."

The pair pushed their way into the suite past several people carrying scripts and tapes into the darkened room not much bigger than an outsize shoebox. Inside was a bank of TV monitors displaying pictures from various different sources. One of them featured a reporter explaining that Carla Wilson was shot in her home and that the police were appealing for anyone who might know something that would explain why. Realising it had slipped her mind, The Stick informed Ben that a Marjorie Wallace had rung.

"Oh God, I had an appointment with her. You explained..."

"Yes, of course, but she wants you to call her whenever you're free."

"Oh God," Ben repeated. "That's all I need."

"Who is she anyway?"

"She's the management butcher who's deciding on where cuts should be made in the news division. She speaks in management code. She talks about 'shooting the puppy' and other such bollocks."

"Oh really, are you worried?"

"We're all worried."

The picture editor, a young man in his 20s, seated at a mixing desk that sported more coloured buttons than an old-fashioned sweetshop, overheard. "Will we be doing the obituary of the obituary department, Ben?"

"Good morning, Jim, how lovely to see you."

Soon, Daniel the arts correspondent arrived and the two began assessing what pictures they had at their disposal and Ben began listing each shot in what looked like an old school exercise book, writing down the time codes for every sequence they thought they might use. A producer was despatched to interview the Head of News and she returned 15 minutes later suggesting they use the second answer. Quickly, Ben worked out a structure involving Carla reporting on a battle raging in Afghanistan, filming Kurdish refugees in Iraq, broadcasting a piece-to-camera at the site of a massacre in Chechnya, and another while police smashed their way into a house during an early morning drugs raid in Manchester. They found the shots of her dancing with Bruce Forsyth, they had the tribute and footage of her playing with animals at Bristol zoo on a special news report about how animals there were being deliberately poisoned. This sequence was the perfect way to end the piece. They still awaited the results of the librarian's search for a sound clip of Carla herself. Daniel linked them together with a crisp, minimal script giving sparse biographical details in the process that he gleaned from various bits of agency copy strewn on the small desk to the right of the picture editor. They included the fact that only three weeks ago she had announced her engagement to a Greek man named Costas and there were pictures of the couple together arriving in a stretch limousine at the premiere of a film about Kosovo from where Carla had reported during the troubles there.

"There's the murderer," said the picture editor gazing up at the footage. "It's always the relative or the lover."

"How can you say that?" The Stick was pleading for the accused from the back of the room.

"Besides, he's well fit."

The picture editor laughed. It was the only moment of levity in a tense edit. News producers were constantly rushing in to check its progress. Dan, microphone in hand, fed script lines one at a time so that the package could be cut piecemeal while new pictures were located. The edit was delayed slightly when the librarian appeared with a clip of a fresh-faced Carla talking about the surprise she had felt when she was first given the job as a foreign correspondent. It was perfect and Dan had to re-adjust his script in order to accommodate it. The edit was all going swimmingly until they were three-quarters through cutting the piece. Suddenly and without warning, the lights on the editing desk went out. The expletives from Jim, the picture editor, would have made a hardened trooper blush. The suite had, like Carla, died. Any ripostes about obituaries for edit suites would probably have tipped Jim over the edge. There were only five minutes to go before the bulletin was due to begin. Jim rushed out to requisition a new edit suite. A young producer cutting something for a future news programme was unceremoniously turfed out of the adjacent one while Ben and Dan sat nervously waiting for Jim to reprogramme it for the resumption of their edit. The news bulletin began. There were several items preceding theirs: a live interview with the reporter at the scene who explained that Carla had been working on a series about street gangs in east London, a vox-pop with neighbours from the street in which she lived and an interview with the Home Secretary. With two items to go before the obit was due, the gallery politely asked why they hadn't put the green light on indicating that the piece was completed. Ben explained the problem and that he still expected it to be ready. The clip of Carla was inserted leaving only the zoo shots to go. They could not find the zoo shots. They were on a tape and had not been fed into the computer server.

"Where are the fucking zoo shots?"

"Where the fuck are they?"

"Oh my God," said The Stick clutching her face. "Some woman came in asking for a headline shot and I gave them to her. She was supposed to bring them straight back."

Without comment, Ben rushed out to the graphics area next door where he discovered the headline producer sauntering nonchalantly in his direction with the required tape. Ben grabbed it, smiling ruefully at her while he did so. With one item only before they were due on air, the gallery was getting nervous. The Stick was chewing her fingernails, which were longer than her teeth. "Edit 1, I still see no green. What's going on?" The director's concerned voice was blaring through the intercom. Jim pushed the tape into the machine before answering the gallery. "Just one edit to do."

"Edit 1, I have to know now. I can delay your piece to the end of the bulletin. Tell me, are you going to make it?"

"Yes, yes, we'll be OK," shouted Jim though Ben was desperately worried that he wouldn't. The previous item was ending and the presenter was screaming as to which introduction he should read out next.

"Are you ready edit 1?" screamed the director.

"We'll be OK. Read our cue."

The newsreader began reading the introduction that Ben had crafted diligently before the edit had begun. Jim pressed one button, then another. Nothing seemed to happen. Ben looked alarmed. Jim pressed it again. It worked this time. He pressed the green button. "Go, go, go," he screamed. There was a collective exhaling of breath. It was as close a run thing as you could get but they had made their slot. Jim looked surprisingly calm. This sort of thing happened fairly regularly with late breaking stories though not often quite as tight as in this case. The deodorant that Ben had applied after his shower that morning had just about held its own though the anti-perspirant element had long given up the ghost. A guilt-ridden Stick was holding back tears. Buoyed by their success, Ben cupped her cheeks in both hands and gave them an affectionate rub. That only brought on a stream of relief.

There were thanks all round at the post-bulletin briefing with a couple more suggestions of material to be used in the succeeding versions. As Ben accompanied The Stick back to his office, he could feel his heart rate decreasing. He waved away her flow of apologies and diverted her by asking what she'd learned about the production process.

"Telly is primarily all about pictures, Stick, just as radio is mostly about audio. I didn't bother making an obit of JD Salinger, you know the man who wrote Catcher in the Rye because the man was publicity shy and there was no video of him other than a few seconds of poor quality amateur footage that the copyright holders wanted an absurd amount of money for permission to use. Likewise, Keith didn't bother creating a radio obit of the great French mime artist Marcel Marceau for obvious reasons. Actually I'm wrong. Keith made an obit of Marcel Marceau with the soundtrack of John Cage's opus, '4 minutes 33 seconds'." The Stick nodded though she hadn't a clue what he was talking about. When they reached the office and opened the door, Anthony was putting the finishing touches to the pictures that accompanied his website text and Keith, wearing overlarge headphones that gave him the appearance of having landed from a remote corner of some far-distant universe, was cursing at his computer which, as he put it, couldn't save a life let alone his feature.

"How's it going?" Ben asked Anthony.

With an exaggerated press of a button on his keyboard, the answer was "Gone".

"Well done, good work all round no doubt."

"How did yours go?"

The Stick looked at Ben.

"Well, it was the best we could do in the circumstances," he said

"Did you find a decent ending?"

"Not really, a bit of her playing with some orangutans. I expect there'll be a few aaaggghhhs either because she's dead or because the monkeys looked sweet."

"Don't be cynical," said The Stick, her eyes red.

"Talking of monkeys..." Ben walked over to the office monkey. "My honours this time?" Without waiting for an answer the button was pressed and the shrieking began until another touch of the button brought it to an end.

"When you've got time, Sticky, I want you, as an exercise, to look out more pictures of Carla, ones that we didn't have time to look at, to see how much we could have improved our effort by if we'd had the time. Alright?"

"Alright, boss."

Ben turned towards Keith who had risen to join the others on their side of the room. "Yours go alright, Keith?"

"Yes, I expect I said much the same as you. I did mention though that she was dyslexic and that she had to memorise each line of her scripts before she delivered them because she had trouble reading them."

"Well I never knew that."

"Did you know that, Anthony?"

"Yep, but only 'cos Keith told me."

"I also know that she had an abortion when she was 17," added Keith.

"You didn't put that in, did you?" asked The Stick looking concerned.

"Of course not."

"Was it yours?" asked Anthony.

"No it wasn't."

"So do you ever put anything private in?" asked The Stick.

"Only if there's a relevance," replied Keith. "If she had started campaigning against the abortion law, then it becomes relevant. She'd be a hypocrite. Otherwise it's no more admissible than saying she suffered from haemorrhoids."

"So if she walked about with her legs wide apart like this when she was doing her reports, then you could mention her piles," said The Stick, with a contorted expression, ambling about the room like a cowboy who'd dismounted his horse after three solid weeks in the saddle. Even Anthony couldn't help laughing.

"I see you've recovered from your trauma," said Ben.

"So who do you reckon might have killed poor old Carla then?" asked Keith as the laughter subsided. Before anyone could answer, his phone rang again. It was Marjorie Wallace.

"Ben, I know you've been pushing your bandwith today but now that your piece has gone out, I think it's the perfect time to come and touch base and maybe join me in an ideas shower. Would you mind? It should only take a few minutes."

"What, right now?"

"If you wouldn't mind."

Ben had expected Marjorie Wallace to be installed in some grand office full of mahogany, fancy paintings and pot plants. Instead, she sat at a modest desk in the corner of an open-plan office in which seven or eight people, mostly women, sat typing at their terminals. Marjorie was in her mid to late thirties, too young to be called Marjorie and much younger than Ben, which gave him a measure of confidence. She was smart, formal, and Ben thought, "how many times do I have to defend myself to upstarts like you?" After a cursory chat about the murder and whether or not Ben knew Carla well, they got down to the main business.

"Ben, let's swallow the frog," she said, straightening her posture. "As you know we are having to implement our downsizing policy in the division."

"Cut jobs, yes."

"Let me put this to you, Ben. I've just watched your obituary broadcast, one that hadn't been prepared beforehand and the result was perfectly creditable. So it begs the question, 'Do we need a dedicated obituary producer?' Ben looked at Marjorie for a moment. His mind was racing, the adrenaline that had subsided only minutes ago had returned to its previous level. Was this the most inopportune moment to mount a defence, he wondered? Not at all. Hadn't he just been talking to the Women's Institute about this only hours earlier in a speech he knew off by heart?

"We were lucky, Marjorie. Carla was a BBC employee and because of that we had piles of footage of her stored in our archive. But what if it had been someone equally famous from the commercial sector say who'd been shot? Or a famous celebrity, someone not in our employ? Sure, we'd be able to cobble something together quickly like we did this afternoon but you'd notice the difference. It can often take days to sort through programmes trying to find the best footage or the most appropriate clips – those dramatic openings or endings that leave you with a tear in the eye."

Marjorie listened intently and then began writing notes in a small pad.

"Let me give you some examples of those endings I'm talking about. Do you remember the renowned judge Lord Denning?" Marjorie nodded.

"I found a clip in which he quoted King Alfred, who he was named after." Ben then imitated Denning's famous Hampshire brogue. "I long to leave to the men that came after, a remembrance of me in good works, a remembrance of me in good works. That's how I'd like to be remembered."

Ben looked at Marjorie and wasn't sure if she was mesmerised or fearful. He continued what amounted to a performance.

"Then there was the society photographer Norman Parkinson who took many of the most famous shots of the Royal Family. I found these words of his in an interview made at his home on the island of Tobago." Ben then affected an upper-class accent.

"We have a private burial ground here because I couldn't bear to be buried with people I hadn't been introduced to. So if you want to come and see me with a cairn on my chest and maybe a pretty tree, that's where you'll find me."

Marjorie remained deadpan, silent and gazing straight at him. Ben was convinced, however, that if he hadn't already won her round, he soon would.

"When the former Lord Chancellor, Lord Hailsham was asked how he'd like to be remembered, he replied, 'I shall throw myself on the mercy of the court.' And what about Sir John Gielgud? I ended his obituary with a recitation from The Tempest: 'We are such stuff as dreams are made on, and our little life is rounded with a sleep.' At this point a curtain is pulled across his face. Now, I tell you, Marjorie, what better ways to end these obits? And I can assure you that if any old newsroom producer had had to cobble them together in the way I did this afternoon with Carla Wilson, we'd have certainly missed these gems because the chances are he or she would not have been given the time to sift through all the silt to discover those pearls. To get rid of the dedicated obituaries department would be a genuine case of dumbing down and it would only take an example of a ragged royal obit or some such to have the wrath of the Daily Mail and any other anti-BBC organ, in parliament say, to come crashing down on us. I rest my case."

Marjorie paused, smiled and congratulated Ben on his performance.

"You've certainly pushed the needle in your position, I can see that."

Ben groaned inwardly. After a brief discussion on the roles of the other members of his team, she thanked him for coming. On her notebook Ben noticed the words Hailsham, Parkinson, Denning and Gielgud. He said goodbye and strode out of the office. A woman he didn't know sitting nearby smiled at him as he passed.

"I don't think we'll be hearing from Mrs Wallace again," Ben announced confidently as he walked into the office and pacifying the concerned expressions. "I think we've climbed her strategic staircase," he said raising his eyes. As he spoke, he noticed on the balcony outside their window an elderly man with a net trying to recapture a fugitive parrot. It transpired that the bird had escaped from the filming of a children's programme. It was that sort of a day.

3 STEVE

"As a result of the overcrowding due to the short-forming of this train, we will be non-stopping at the next station."

The tannoy announcement was the catalyst that tipped an already angry Steve Graham into a paroxysm of disgust. He looked at Robbie Blake who stood inches away from him as they formed a throng in the middle of the carriage, surveying the lucky ones who'd managed to secure a seat while they had insufficient room even to remove their coats without causing a disturbance.

"It's not enough that they nearly crush us to death in this fucking Black Hole of Calcutta, it's not enough that the train left 15 minutes late, now they assault us with bad grammar as well."

"Like you're assaulting us with your bad language you mean," intoned Hilary calmly as she stood on his other side without raising her eyes from her book.

"At least my bad language is grammatically correct."

"Oh, that's alright then."

Steve continued unabashed.

"I mean, short-formed for God's sake. Mickey Rooney's short-formed. Or Frankie Detorri. Not a fucking train."

Robbie smiled.

"As for non-stopping. I suppose if the bloody train doesn't turn up at all it's non-formed."

"Are you non-happy, Steve?" Hilary ventured.

"Too bloody right I'm non-happy. You pay thousands of pounds, more than anywhere else in the world for a crap rail system on which you can't get a seat. What's more, getting a seat isn't even part of the bloody contract. We're made to feel grateful for standing room only while the first-class carriages are half empty and those bastard bosses who've administered decades of under investment, botched privatisation and who couldn't tell a good train service from a bucket of shit pocket six-figure bonuses." It had become a rant. "You know, some pip squeak from one of the rail companies said the other day that overcrowding is done deliberately to stop more people using the service to make it more fucking manageable. I ask you. In other words while we stand here cramped up like sardines in a tin, we're actually performing a public service by deterring others from taking the train. So by making the service more efficient, the rail bosses will get a bigger bonus. QED. If it wasn't for the fact that I can't afford to live in the capital and driving to work would be even worse, I'd be a non-commuter that's for fucking sure."

There was a pause while everybody concurred without saying anything. Robbie broke the silence.

"Has commuting left you non-plussed, Steve?"

There were a few chuckles even from those not acquainted with this group of friends yet whose faces were instantly recognisable by the sheer routine of spending hours together in their metal projectile. Somehow the travails of commuting, particularly on a bad day such as this, bound commuters together in a common siege mentality.

"I certainly ain't plussed, that's for sure," replied Steve at last managing to raise a smile.

"Why is it I have to be crushed up against you Robbie? Why couldn't I have been sharing this enforced intimacy with Hilary?"

"Less of the sexism please," Hilary responded still without averting her eyes from her book that she was still able to read quite happily despite the mass of humanity engulfing her.

"Where's Ben this morning?" asked Steve. "Still getting over that dreadful shooting I expect. Did he know the woman?"

"Not very well, apparently," Hilary answered. "What a terrible business." There were general groans of agreement.

"In answer to your question, I passed Ben on the way in trying to put his chain back on again," said Robbie.

"Again! Christ, the guy's a walking liability," Steve responded.

"A riding liability," suggested Robbie.

"Right first time," said Hilary.

There was an audible click and the sound of breathing as the tannoy announcer prepared to impart another message.

"Here we go, another blast of non-grammar to cheer us all up," moaned Steve.

"We'd like to apologise for the late running of this train. This was due to the late arrival of the driver. We do apologise for any inconvenience caused."

"Oh yeah, as if they really care," mumbled Steve, amid a general moan from the carriage's occupants.

Steve's thoughts were brought down to earth suddenly as the train came to a shuddering halt out in the countryside away from any station.

"Jesus Christ, what now?"

The level of humdrum suddenly increased as the commuters began to share their dissatisfaction and the inconveniences the delay would incur on their day. Their frustration was heaped upon a hapless member of the railway staff who was walking down the train towards the driver's compartment to determine why the train had stopped. Luckily for him, the general mood was lifted when a middle-aged woman harangued him with the words, "This train is supposed to be a public convenience." Steve would probably have collapsed on the floor laughing had there been any space. Even the railway man chuckled. "I think you'll find the public convenience is in the next carriage down, Madam."

As the laughter subsided, someone pointed out a railway employee walking alongside the stationary train holding a stick. The ensuing curiosity was answered as the click of the tannoy presaged another announcement. It came in the manner of a flight attendant who might have been pointing out that if we looked hard enough we might see the Grand Canyon below.

"Ladies and gentlemen, the reason for our delay is visible on the left hand side of the train where a bull has strayed on to the line."

"Well, I thought I'd heard them all," Steve remarked as scores of embattled commuters diverted their gaze towards the window. Sure enough, there was the large black creature jauntily strutting his stuff up the slow track as if it had been released into a Spanish bullring. It had found its way through a hedge and clambered up the levée and on to the railway. Camera phones began clicking, tweets were twittered and inevitably, there were cries of "Olė" from some of the men, "Ah bless" from the women.

"Wrong kind of cow on the line," suggested Robbie. One passenger, who claimed to have once lived in the country, was sure it was a young bull. "A short stick's the best way to get a bull to obey you," Robbie suggested to Steve.

"Didn't know you were a country boy, Robbie?"

"I'm not. Heard it on The Archers."

The bull began trotting at a brisker pace as the man with the stick tried to keep up.

"Shouldn't he be holding a red cape?" asked one of the throng.

Someone else told a joke about a bull which provoked several more. Hilary's caused the most amusement. "What's the difference between a bull and The James Last Orchestra? The bull has horns at the front and an arsehole at the back."

"I hope they don't kill it," said one woman.

"If they do, you can write its obituary, Steve," said Hilary.

It was no coincidence that Steve Graham was also an obituary writer who shared the same train as another obituarist most mornings. For some five years, he had sat opposite Ben and listened to him alleviate the drudgery of the morning commute with his titbits of information about a famous actor, politician, TV celebrity or whomsoever Ben happened to be working on that particular week. It only augmented Steve's enthusiasm for the juicy lives in which he immersed himself when reading the obituary columns in the newspapers including the one for which he wrote, *The National Herald*, where he'd worked previously on the sports desk for five years. He loved reading about the major who would go into the fiercest of battles carrying an umbrella in case it rained, or the woman who survived all manner of atrocities in concentration camps to become a star of horror films and dubbed "the most beautiful ghoul in the world", the Austrian whistler who had a sex-change or the wife of a media magnate who believed every good wife should suck her husband's toes. So, when a rare vacancy in his own obituaries department arose, Steve jumped at the chance.

"Did you know, Robbie, that that business about the bull focusing on the colour red in a bullfight is a myth. Bulls are colour blind and the tradition of having a red cape began because they wanted to hide the blood."

"Is that a fact? How come you're so well informed on bullfighting?"

"When I was a sports writer the paper sent me to Madrid once to report on some English matador who was making it big there. El Higginbotham or some ridiculous name or other. It wasn't my idea. There aren't many sports I can't get to like if I try hard enough, but bullfighting is not one of them."

"But isn't it a wonderful spectacle – all that colour, pageantry and all those trumpets..."

"Yes of course it is until the action starts and they begin taunting the bulls by spearing them and driving them crazy. I know that the crowd gets all excited by the different moves the matador makes..."

"What do they call them, paso doble or something?" asked Robbie.

Steve paused. He began to smirk.

"No, I don't think it's a paso doble, Robbie. I think the bull would need to get up on its hind legs for a paso doble." As he chuckled, so Robbie began laughing at himself in a series of snorts that might have come from a dancing bull. Once he'd recovered he asked Steve if he missed going to all those sporting occasions.

"Not at all. I got fed up with being sent to damp, cold football grounds miles from home reporting on dull middle-of-the-table matches. Don't get me wrong, I love my football. I played it a bit at university when I wasn't marching against some form of injustice or other. And I've been a loyal supporter of Grimsby Town. But I love the characters, the virtuosi, the water carriers, the managers, the umpires, the referees, the commentators, all that stuff. But more and more I had to write about the big-business side of the game, which I detest, and the spot-fixing scandals in cricket and the corruption in boxing. Aside from that, editors are always playing the blame game – who was at fault here, who should we blame for that defeat, that crowd problem, the perpetual underperformance of English teams. In the end, they wanted sports writers to be sociologists. I just got bored, Robbie."

As Robbie nodded, and the train started to move again, Steve's thoughts harked back to his childhood. He remembered sitting in his bedroom for hours during summer nights when sleep was elusive playing imaginary cricket by way of a game he invented using playing cards. He would write out the teams of all the international cricketers of the day and sometimes, if he couldn't remember enough of them, would make them up. As a result, players like Poppadom, Biriyani, Korma and Bhaji would grace the batting and bowling ranks of the subcontinent Test sides. He would compile their averages assiduously. It was an entirely singular pursuit. An only child, he never shared his enthusiasm with either of his parents especially as both had, at some time or other, expressed concern that he was spending far too much dreaming of playing at Sabina Park, Jamaica or Eden Gardens, Calcutta when he should be paying more attention to his homework. He would lock himself into this fantasy world and could become most disgruntled when mundane interruptions such as the need to eat would impinge upon his dream world.

"The other thing, Robbie, was that I felt the longer I stayed as a sports writer, the more I would get type-cast. So after listening to the fun Ben was having I decided that was the job for me, so when an obit vacancy came up I leapt at the chance."

Steve didn't mention to Robbie that another factor in leaving sport was to save his marriage. His wife, Maria, had grown increasingly upset at the amount of time he spent away from home and suspected that her husband's many nights in provincial hotels were not always unaccompanied. Steve remembered the strenuous preparations he had undertaken to secure the appointment in the obits department. He ensured that the editor there became aware of a hinterland beyond the cricket pitch and the football field. He began to lace his match reports with pretentious political and literary references. Quotations from Shakespeare and Milton were often sprinkled into his copy. References to Greek, Roman and even Icelandic mythology occasionally found a place.

He had approached his interview for the obits job with a near-obsessional alacrity. He devoured as many books on obituaries he could find. He learnt that the reporting of death had gone on for centuries.

The Greeks would eulogise about fallen heroes, and throughout history victims of wars and battles, at least in the officer class, have been described in often-gory detail. Steve learnt too that the British Library housed collections of The Gentleman's Magazine, an extraordinary publication from the 18th century that comprised everything from learned essays on historical events and foreign affairs, to poetry, gardening tips and commodity prices. In particular, its later editions contained the first examples of the modern obituary form by including anecdote with biographical detail. In the midst of the announcement of the deaths of establishment figures as soldiers, clerics, public figures and suchlike, Steve came across surprising gems including this rather tragic example.

" At an hotel in Glasgow, aged 30, Miss Jessie Lauder of a respectable family in Edinburgh, who committed suicide from disappointed love. She appears to have written to her lover a few days previously, and a letter, which the servant girl took up to the deceased's room when she found her dead, was an answer to it. He apologises for the delay in writing to her, and ascribes this delay to her letter having been missent to a town three miles distant from his proper address in proof of which he encloses the envelope marked 'Missent to G-----."

It was the kind of miserable episode, he thought, that might have inspired an author such as Thomas Hardy. At the subsequent job interview, for which he dressed entirely in black, a detail not lost on the panel, Steve impressed its members with his background knowledge and enthusiasm for the obituary form. He got off to a risky start. When the news editor asked him what he thought was the most essential ingredient to a well-written obituary, he replied, "Ensure the subject is dead." He then expounded on some of the better-known personalities despatched prematurely in print. Contrary to popular opinion, he pointed out that Mark Twain's oft-misquoted example did not in fact appear in an obituary. The reality was that in 1897 a journalist was sent to his home to investigate a false report that the author was on death's door. Twain then recounted in the New York Journal "The report of my death is an exaggeration." Steve went on to describe how authors in particular seemed to be vulnerable to being written off before their time. The poet Samuel Taylor Coleridge received an obituary after a man found hanged in London's Hyde Park was wearing a shirt bearing his name. It turns out the shirt had most likely been stolen by the victim. Robert Graves' obit appeared in The Times when it believed wrongly that he had been fatally wounded at the Battle of the Somme in 1916. When Rudyard Kipling's death was incorrectly announced in a magazine, the author wrote to its editor saying, "I've just read that I'm dead. Don't forget to delete me from your list of subscribers." Steve could have listed several other figures that provided amusement after being written off before their time. When the obituary of folk musician Dave Swarbrick of Fairport Convention fame was published in the Daily Telegraph, he is said to have remarked, "It's not the first time I've died in Coventry." After a mock obituary of rock musician Alice Cooper in Melody Maker magazine was taken seriously by some fans, Cooper issued a statement saying, "I'm alive and drunk as usual." When Le Figaro mistakenly printed the obituary of Alfred Nobel, who had made his fortune after patenting dynamite, it described him as a man of whom it would be difficult to describe as a benefactor to humanity. It's said that reading it shocked Nobel into leaving his vast wealth for the setting up of a foundation that would award prizes for literature, science and peace. And a whole raft of pre-written obituaries of world leaders were published by mistake on the CNN website in 2003. Using Queen Elizabeth the Queen Mother as a template, somehow the obits became garbled so that former US Vice-president Dick Cheney was described as "the UK's favourite grandmother", the Pope enjoyed "a love of racing" and Fidel Castro had been "a lifeguard, athlete and movie star". On the other hand, reading his own premature obituary is said to have caused the actual death of the Black Nationalist Marcus

Garvey. The Chicago Defender, mistakenly believing he had passed away, described him as having died "broke, alone and unpopular" and reading it aloud, Garvey emitted a loud moan, collapsed with a stroke and died the following day.

Steve's thoughts were momentarily distracted by another train hold up. Some excuse followed about being stuck behind another train on the slow lane until the announcement came that it would be "all steam ahead from now on".

"All steam ahead? I'm told the trains all ran on time in the bloody steam age."

When asked if there was any way he thought he could improve the Herald's obituary coverage, Steve suggested looking towards North America for an answer. He was aware that in the US and Canada many of the local or regional newspapers/websites had given over space to the obits of ordinary people who had an interesting story to tell. Whereas the run-of- the-mill obituary in the British broadsheets dealt with the career achievements and the public face of its subjects, the Americans delved more deeply into private lives, not necessarily in terms of who they'd slept with, but by way of the colour, the taste, the smell of living an ordinary life in perhaps an extraordinary way. They focused much more on the character details of often-small town folks; the cars they drove, the cigarettes they smoked, the mannerisms they exhibited, their brashness, arrogance, dignity, their love and sometimes their hate, capturing the essence of the private man or woman. "Yes, some of the writing might be over-sentimental for a UK readership," he pleaded, "but written in the house-style they're the kind of real life stories that everybody will go for, believe me." It would be unfair to say that this idea was the one that sealed Steve's appointment since he was way ahead of the rest of the field in his performance at the interview. But if there was a scintilla of doubt in the mind of any of the interview panel members as to whether Steve was the fit and proper person for the job, the idea of the common-man obit, the type of person with whom Who's Who would not be interested, was the one that removed it.

On being appointed, Steve was given several weeks to prepare for the weekly obituary of the ordinary person. He set about combing the death notices of both national and local papers looking for pointers to an interesting story, such as "all members of the Sauerkraut Society are welcome at the funeral". He networked as best as he could and appealed to readers to offer suggestions as to possible subjects. The department decided after much thought that they wouldn't give it a separate heading but just include it every Friday on the same section of the same page. There was some relaxation for his obits over some of the standard formatting.

"I'm not so bothered about where my subjects went to school for example or when they got married," he argued to his editor, Harry Fearnley, " I'm more interested in what they got up to behind the bike sheds or how they popped the question to their fiancées." Each week Steve informed with his customary light touch and verbal parsimony on such as the Morris dancer from Oxfordshire whose colleague placed a live frog down his trousers while performing the sword dance in front of The Queen, and how, though cursing between clenched teeth, never missed a cue, never missed a step. There was the London bus conductor who arrived in England from the West Indies in the first wave of mass immigration and became famous in her locality for bursting into Trinidadian calypsos during rainy days "to radiate a little sunshine into the drabness". There was the businessman who had little or no formal education but who held a passion for gardening. As a young man he would, for very little money, weed, prune and design the gardens of his neighbours, familiarising himself with what plants grew best in which soils, which thrived in sun or shade, planting each with a particular regard to adjacent colours. As his local reputation grew, his admirers clubbed together in an extraordinary display of community feeling to send him on an expensive landscape gardening course from which he benefited to the extent that when he died his landscaping company employed nearly 30 people. Steve discovered the most unusual subjects too. On one occasion a man emailed him telling him that his wife had died not long after leaving prison for attempting to murder his mistress. The husband wrote giving his side of the story. Steve contacted the children and friends and was given a completely different version of the events. Steve told the tale straight giving both sides. It generated more feedback than any story in the whole of the newspaper that week. His obits became almost cult reading. Steve was flattered to hear a discussion programme on BBC Radio 4 in which someone referred to "the kind of story you read in the *Herald's* Friday obituary page". It wasn't all plain sailing though. There was one obituary in particular, that was to cause him much grief further down the line.

In the meantime, the train had advanced further down its line and the relief of Steve and the other passengers of reaching their destination and being disgorged from near-suffocation was palpable.

4 ROBBIE

It was after listening to Robbie relating on the 8.25 a key moment in his life that Steve first thought of writing true stories, later refining his idea to writing "real-life" obituaries once he'd studied the North American model. Robbie's tale exemplified the randomness of life, how a slight jerk of the puppet string by the hand of destiny can influence the direction in which the world takes one. Curiously, his story was to have an even more direct influence on Steve's own life later on in a way no one could possibly have predicted. 10 or so years before, Robbie Blake had been on his way home during the evening crush on the London tube. As he neared the top of the escalator, his torpid state of mind brought on by the weariness of a hard day's labour was jolted back to the noisy reality around him. A young woman in a bright yellow raincoat about his age, late 20s, brushed past him in a seemingly desperate hurry, nearly causing him to lose his balance. His irritation turned to *schadenfreude* as the woman managed to get herself trapped in the ticket barrier. She had entered it before the rear pincers had closed from the previous user but not before the front ones had clamped shut. As she shot into the mechanism, she dropped her ticket while trying to insert it. Robbie, who was about to place his ticket into the machine, picked hers up and fed in his, thus releasing her from her entrapment as the second set of jaws clanged open. She, in turn, removed the ticket and quickly melted into the maelstrom of the rush hour. But before she disappeared, she did something that so affected him that he didn't notice in time that the tickets had got mixed up and that each was now in possession of the other's. It was simply the look that she gave him that, in a matter of seconds, completely transfixed him, dispelling any lingering sense of antagonism.

It was simply a look but it was a look that was anything but simple, at least not to him. Not surprisingly, her expression was initially apologetic. She had after all held up the current of people negotiating their way through these metal obstacles causing a momentary ripple in the wrong direction. There was the blush of embarrassment at the way she'd been caught out by her undue haste, leaving her stranded between those two metallic pincers. There was an element of surprise, surprise that this had happened to her for the first time in years of passing through these same gates. Guilt permeated her too for having found herself ensconced in a predicament that could so easily have been avoided had she not been so pushy in the literal sense. She looked helpless as her ticket dropped to the floor, unable to retrieve it given her temporary imprisonment. But above all, what struck Robbie so acutely was how all these elements of her demeanour suddenly transformed into such a beautiful smile of gratitude that it took his breath away. There was something about her warmth that touched his heart, the shape of her perfect teeth, the wide gaze of her dark eyes.

Her image was emblazoned in his mind in the way he'd visualise portrait paintings at which he'd spent many an hour gazing in galleries in London and elsewhere in Europe. He could marvel at the delicate brushwork of an El Greco or a Titian. He could appreciate the historical context of a Goya or a Rembrandt, or the religious symbolism of the Renaissance painters. But what always detained him that extra minute or so was interpreting facial expressions. To Robbie, this was the aspect he enjoyed most about visual art. He remembered once being taken on a primary school trip to London's Wallace Collection where Frans Hals's Laughing Cavalier hung. "Look closely everyone and tell me if you think the cavalier is really laughing," the teacher, Mrs Wilmot, had said. For the first time he was made to give a picture more than a surface glance. He determined that though his eyes were "smiling", the expression was nevertheless more of a kind of caddish smugness than one of joy, rather like the look that Tony Bradshaw gave when he was bullying people in the school playground. From that moment on, whenever he visited a gallery, he would be attracted most by portraits. One of Robbie's favourite works was Goya's Portrait of Isabel Lobo Porcel at the National. Each time he viewed it he would lose himself in the sultriness of her face, contemplating what might be the thoughts behind her dark, almost cavernous eyes.

Robbie imagined, as he sat down on the train a few minutes later, a conversation in which he commissioned from a master artist a portrait such as the one that now dominated his thoughts. "Mr Goya, could you knock me up an expression with a hint of embarrassment mixed in with apology, add a touch of surprise and a soupcon of guilt and top it off with a good dose of gratitude." It would never have sufficed. The image of the girl in the yellow raincoat had stirred something within him that he couldn't comprehend. This was his Isabel, except that she was a living and breathing person somewhere out there. He simply couldn't get her out of his mind. It got to the point where he began questioning himself. Why had such a silly incident affected him so? Would she have even thought twice about it? Was it taking on an undue prominence because of a deep down sense of loneliness?

Robbie had cut a lonely figure ever since the death of his mother when he was 16. The two had been close and, as an only child, he had never had to contend with sibling rivalry, though he often longed for a brother or sister. His mother had been not only his main emotional support but had encouraged in him an interest in the arts and other worldly pursuits. As a child, she would insist on regular trips to the local children's theatre and to the cinema while his father worked hard to build up an insurance broking business. Robbie would accompany her, at first grudgingly, to museums and galleries but she would always ensure that the visits were short and as much fun as she could make them. He would tell her about his day at school because she wanted to hear it, chiding him if she felt he was being unfair to his playmates or to the teachers. Robbie's relationship with his father was typically more distant. Mr Blake while not discouraging Robbie's artistic interests was more interested in pursuits such as rugby, rugby and rugby. He was certainly in no way uncaring but whereas his wife, Martha, held a more enlightened view when it came to emotional development, Henry Blake was still somewhat distrustful of too much of what he called "showiness" where boys were concerned.

So when Martha succumbed to cancer in a short space of time, it wasn't just Robbie who found himself all at sea. Henry had to fulfil a role for which he was ill prepared. What made it more difficult was that Robbie was at that awkward stage of adolescence when everything in the world was “stupid”. He was a long time in denial; mothers, he thought, didn’t die when you still needed looking after. When she finally succumbed, he took her death hard, developing anger that he directed towards himself, rendering him emotionally shrink-wrapped. He began drinking heavily on Saturday nights out with his friend Richard and his schoolwork suffered. He and his father became regularly confrontational, locking horns like rutting stags, often reducing Robbie to tears though seldom in view. Eventually, his father, feeling that he needed stability, persuaded Robbie to join the insurance firm. It had always been the last thing he’d ever wanted to do, but he’d always been good with figures and he’d become worn-down by arguments that he was sailing rudderless through choppy waters and needed a firm direction to his life. He had no mother to turn to for help. His father at least ensured that he got the best training from the right people, though not from him; that would have been too risky.

Eventually, things settled down as routine took hold and within three years he could afford a mortgage on a small flat with the help of the deposit from his father. He’d had several girlfriends but none had lasted more than a year. Somehow, in the deep recesses of his mind had come the notion that his mother would not have thought any of them worthy. He was projecting his own instincts of course and at the same time he was forming an increasing alienation to his profession. Though he was progressing well, he felt more and more that he chose it merely out of necessity. In fact, it had been chosen for him. The only creative direction in which the insurance business seemed to be heading was to find ever more ingenious ways of exploiting potential clients’ fears.

Robbie stared at the ticket, her ticket. Like his, it was a rail season ticket, beginning from a station not too far from his though on a different line. He knew that if he handed it in, the train company could trace her address and return it to her. Perhaps she would do that with his. Or maybe she would just steal it because there were more months pending on it, though judging from the warmth of her smile, he doubted she was that type. He decided that for a couple of days at least he would arrive some 20 minutes before the time he'd encountered her, judging that she'd been dashing for a train that day. He wanted to see her again; something told him he must. Certainly everybody he'd mentioned it to egged him on to do so. But would he recognise her? Was he romanticising her look in his mind? If he did meet her, would she smile, thank him and just leave? Why wouldn't she? Someone like her was bound to have a boyfriend or a husband or a partner. Wouldn't he be risking deep disappointment? He was calling her Isabel and wondered if her real name might be Gladys or Beryl or something else far less enchanting.

He was still questioning the idea as he rode up the same escalator the following day, staring down at the metallic grooved stairs that meshed with the framework before disappearing at the top. As he stepped off and looked up, to his enormous surprise, she was there at the barrier. He spotted her yellow raincoat several metres away. She was holding his ticket aloft in her hand trying to draw attention to the hundreds of people streaming past but he would have recognised her anyway. He was holding her ticket too, and to spare her any embarrassment in case she didn't recognise him he held hers up in the same way. The moment of recognition provoked in her a squeal of excitement and another smile that seemed to melt away his nervousness. There followed an animated exchange about how the tickets managed to get swapped, how embarrassed she felt for causing the problem and, from him, how silly it was that she should feel this way. They laughed at their both having the idea about going back to the tube station at the same time and worrying about not recognising each other and what they'd have done if they hadn't. When there was a pause and each not quite knowing what to say next, he ventured, "Fancy a drink?" "Why not," she replied with scarcely a pause and there began the relationship that changed Robbie's life.

bulletins. From the early black and white Ealing comedies to his famous TV interpretation of George Smiley in Le Carré's Tinker, Tailor, Soldier, Spy, Ben had lovingly crafted some of Guinness's career highlights. Then, in time for the main evening bulletin, came the news of the death of Sir Robin Day, Britain's well-known political programme anchor. The solution was to lead with Day as the breaking news, and end with the Guinness. "It won't be the last time a Guinness would be taken at the end of a bulletin," Anthony had quipped.

But usually editors won't accommodate two news items commemorating a death. Ben remembered vividly the death of Bernard Miles. Lord Miles was a much-loved actor and theatre owner. He would play Long John Silver annually in Treasure Island at his Mermaid Theatre and was also the voice of at least two popular TV adverts including one for Mackeson beer, the catchline for which went: "It looks good, tastes good and by golly it does you good." His obituary was ready to run on the One O'Clock News, but a live interview overran and Lord Miles was squeezed out. By the time of the Six O'Clock News, the distinguished actress Dame Peggy Ashcroft, who had been in a coma for several days, took her final bow. The editor didn't want two obits in the bulletin, so poor Lord Miles was upstaged at the very end.

"Do you remember Ben that time when we had that young kid, Marcus, from the East End here for a couple of days – learning how to edit radio pieces?" said Keith.

"The super-cool black dude with all the patter, of course I do."

"Well, apparently, he's now running a pirate radio station playing hip-hop and I heard him on the radio the other day saying how he's trying to get people out of gangs to become Deejays instead."

"Yes, I liked him, good sort, if I understood him right."

"He certainly cheered the place up," added Anthony.

"I think I might pay him a visit."

"What on earth for?" asked Ben.

"He lives not far from me. See if there's any word out on the street about Carla?"

"But that's the police's job."

"Won't do any harm. If he knows anything, I'll tell the Old Bill."

"Well watch yourself."

"Yes, boss."

It's intriguing, Ben told The Stick, how famous people of the same profession should die at the same time. Go back nearly two centuries to 1826 and, in the United States, fate decreed that two former presidents should die within hours of each other: John Adams, the nation's second President, and his successor, Thomas Jefferson. There was a certain paradox about this coincidence since, though the pair had worked together for the cause of independence, once in government they became bitter political enemies. It was fitting that the date of their deaths should be none other than 4 July, the 50th anniversary of American independence.

Spool back a couple more centuries, to 23 April 1616, and another significant event took place, this time in the literary arena. It was the day William Shakespeare, to use his own phrase, shuffled off this mortal coil. But he didn't have the limelight all to himself, Ben explained. Miguel de Cervantes, of Don Quixote fame, had also exited, stage left, only hours before. Strictly speaking, some say that because dates in England and Spain were then configured by different calendars, Cervantes actually died a day earlier. But if ever there was a case for poetic licence, this was it.

Ben explained to an attentive Stick that sometimes, the deaths of the distinguished can be overshadowed by the simultaneous demise of an even more famous individual. The obvious examples of this were the two authors CS Lewis and Aldous Huxley, who died on 22 November 1963 – the day John F Kennedy was assassinated. If you wanted to go quietly, this was the perfect day. It has often been remarked that the death of Mother Teresa was denied its due momentousness by the fact that all the shocked world's eyes were on the funeral of Princess Diana who had died five days earlier. Spare a thought, Ben added, for the family of Sir Georg Solti, the conductor who shared his death day with the so-called Angel of Calcutta.

Ben also explained how a person's worth has little bearing on their popularity or celebrity. For example, among Ben's losing battles to have his obituaries aired were the famous Russian cellist Mstislav Rostropovich (not mainstream enough and, besides, Russian) though he won with Alexandr Solzhenitsyn (equally Russian but a bit more mainstream). Other factors can help persuade an editor. Solzhenitsyn wrote books that were made into films and it helps a TV package enormously if a film clip with a famous actor can illuminate an author's work. But famous actors with memorable film clips don't always do the trick. Among Ben's biggest and disappointing defeats included Rod Steiger. Despite an eventful life and several groundbreaking mainstream films dealing with weighty social issues, such as On the Waterfront, The Pawnbroker and In the Heat of the Night, Rod Steiger's obituary did not run because the editor of the day hadn't heard of him. A younger generation raised on Star Wars was not necessarily schooled in Hollywood's back catalogue. The same went for George C. Scott who won an Oscar for Patton but was once again unknown to the editorial team of the day. Even if the present editorial team had known them, none would have run on the day Carla Wilson died.

Keith entered Greville Place, London E1. The soft drizzle that fell was visible against the dim streetlights spaced regularly before the rows of terraced houses. Above him crossed the flyover on which the sound of going-home cars with their red tail lights flashing by dominated the aural spectrum. However, as he approached No. 29, the thud thud of drum and bass was making its presence felt. Keith's spirits rose. It sounded like Marcus might be at home and this impromptu visit would not be fruitless. He climbed the four steps to the front door and there on one of the bells was Marcus's name, not written in pen or pencil but cut out from a business card, black with silver print. He pushed the button. He waited for a half minute or so and when no one appeared he rang the bell again. This time an inside door was opened, a light switched on and through the frosted glass Keith could make out the unmistakeable outline of Marcus's dreadlocks. When he opened the door, the surprise on his face could have doubled the street's luminance.

"Well if I live and breed, if it aint Keef Boswell. Check dat out Bruv, way-one."

Marcus slapped Keith's outstretched hand, laughing loudly as he did so.

"Nice to see you Marcus, sorry to come unexpectedly."

"Aint nuffink, Bruv. Welcome to my drum, come in from de rain."

"Thanks Marcus, are you well?"

"I'm flat-roofin' man but still afloat, innit?"

Marcus was in his thirties, dressed in jeans and, despite the cold weather, a red T-shirt on which was emblazoned a large cannabis leaf. Still laughing out of the unexpected excitement of seeing someone he didn't expect to meet again, he ushered Keith into his studio, where the music was blasting from a bank of speakers. He apologised for the mess. CDs and vinyl records seemed strewn about the room in a way in a scene which, had Tracy Emin been responsible, might have been entered for the Whitbread Prize. Marcus turned the music down and pushed a stack of CDs off a chair in order to give Keith somewhere to sit. They exchanged pleasantries, or at least what Keith assumed to be pleasantries, and memories of the short time Marcus had spent in the office learning about radio production. Marcus related his subsequent career development in pirate radio and burst into more laughter when

Keith told him how he'd heard him talking on the radio about the gangs in his area. It was the cue for Keith to explain the reason for his surprise visit.

"Marcus, you know I was a friend of Carla Wilson, you know the reporter that was murdered the other day."

"Of course, dat dred, Bruv, real swag, specially she bein' so bangin' too, at least for her age. You know, she come to these ends. I seen her with all da film people, innit. She like a sore thumb being so bayden wid dem 110 crepes and chic garms lookin' beast. "

Keith nodded in agreement as if he understood much of anything that Marcus was saying.

"Yes, that's because she was filming a report on the gangs here in the east-end. What I wondered, Marcus, was whether you'd heard any glimmer on the streets about whether anybody here had killed her."

"Bruv, I been talkin' wid some of da hoodies from ends. You know, some of the bad boys would be braggin' if dey was involved. But I aint heard nuffink. Nobody is shook. Nobody is tellin' over. Baggamanz of hoodies from different ends be comin' here for da radio and dere aint no whisper, Bruv. People were biggin' her up. Da beefs in the ends aint wid da older people, wid respeck to you, Keef."

Keith's brain was doing its best to interpret.

"So you've heard nothing."

"Nuffink, Keef. An' everyone I roll wid are sayin' da same, innit, know wha' I mean?"

"Well, thanks Marcus, it was just a thought. Thanks so much for sparing these few minutes." Keith picked up his coat and signalled to leave.

"She was your wifey den, was she, dis Carla WIlson?"

"No, no, we were just colleagues. As a matter of fact, I hadn't seen much of her in the past few years. We lost touch as she climbed up the career ladder and she was mainly based overseas."

"Well, Keef, if you want to get wid lush bitches like Carla it's bait dat you gotta get yourself a shabby suit man. People be bennin' here at your clappin' garms, Bruv."

Marcus dissolved in laughter, and Keith did so too, without knowing precisely why. Marcus walked him to the door and patted him so hard on the back it nearly knocked him through it.

"Great to see you Marcus. You must come and visit us again."

"Thanks, Bruv, and say hi to Anthony and Benny."

"They say hi to you too."

"Cheers, Bruv."

The door closed and Keith walked away, disappointed not to have secured a scoop. Story of his life. However, when he thought again of Marcus, he smiled and shook his head.

10 IRINA

Robbie Blake settled into his seat on the 1900 hours train having placed his coat in the overhead compartment. He didn't take this train as a rule. He had stayed later at work with the intention of meeting his wife Clare who was visiting the capital. Clare, who was now a director of the charity that helped trafficked women, normally worked at its headquarters in Hertfordshire but was supervising the transfer of some women from a temporary refuge in London. The couple's proposed evening out was scuppered though when Robbie's mother-in-law who was looking after their two young children called to say that one had developed an ear infection and Robbie agreed that he should lend support. Robbie squeezed himself between two overweight men either side of him. Although the train was full, he could spot none of his usual travelling companions in the carriage. This was quite normal. Unlike on the journey into work when one would meet one's fellow travellers at more or less the same spot on the platform each day, somehow on the return journey when the numbers waiting for the train were larger, one left it to chance rather than arrange it by design to meet up with other members of one's clique. Robbie invariably followed a different routine on the return journey. If there was no one to chat to on the way into work he would invariably read a book. In this way, he could get through one a fortnight. Robbie reached into his breast pocket and extracted the free evening newspaper that he'd picked up at the station entrance. On return trips invariably he felt too tired to concentrate on literature and would end up either reading the paper or completing the intermediate Sudoku, or occasionally, both. He'd noticed an article about the financial struggles of "the charitable sector" on the front page and since this was his line of work he decided to read it despite what he perceived to be the misuse of the word "charitable" in this case. Neither Ben nor Steve was around to confirm or dispute this contention. As he spread the newspaper on the table in front of him, his phone rang. His ring tone played the theme tune to the film, The Good, The Bad and The Ugly and one or two fellow passengers recognised it and smiled. Robbie returned the smile as he took the call from Clare. The sound that came through his earpiece ripped the smile from his face.

"Robbie, Robbie, there's been a shooting, someone...."Clare was screaming hysterically down the phone until she was cut off as the train entered a tunnel. The 20 seconds or so before the train re-emerged felt like an hour as Robbie, his palms in a cold sweat and his heart pumping, worried that his wife had been shot, raped or suffered some similar fate in what his father had once called the "evil city". When he called her back, Clare was a little calmer and explained that she had been involved in a shooting but that she was alright. Someone though had been killed. Robbie could scarcely believe what he was hearing and promised he would be there as soon as he could. She told him to come to 19 Belvedere Crescent. When he rang his mother-in-law to explain that he wouldn't be able to help her out after all, he kept the reasons vague, just saying that Clare was experiencing some problems at work and needed him to be there. He didn't want to panic her in the way it was panicking him. The train had become a temporary prison as Robbie was forced to travel miles in the wrong direction from where he urgently needed to be.

It was more than two hours before he appeared at the black and white tiled steps of No.19. Police had cordoned off a large area around the building and Robbie could see the forensic team in their white suits, so familiar from TV cop shows, examining the front porch. Clare, tear-diluted mascara smeared over her face, came from a back entrance flanked by two uniformed police officers, and rushed into his arms sobbing. She explained that she was required at the police station a couple of miles away to sign a statement. One of the policemen ushered the pair into a waiting police car and as they drove off, Clare, still whimpering, recounted falteringly to her shocked and incredulous husband the events that had transpired.

Clare, together with a plain-clothed detective from the Metropolitan Police, were accompanying two Nigerian girls from the women's refuge in Belvedere Crescent to a new purpose-built centre outside of London.

The girls had managed to escape the clutches of an Albanian gang and had gone to the police to tell their story and give details of their captors. There had been some sightings of suspicious looking people hanging around outside the house in recent days and it was felt that the transfer should take place as soon as possible. They emerged from the building along with an old lady, Irina Lockyer, who helped out in the refuge and who was on her way home. As the group began descending the steps, a saloon car roared up on the opposite side of the road and a burst of automatic gunfire came crack crack crack crack crack from the passenger seat. In what Clare described as an utterly surreal scene that appeared to be played out in slow motion, everyone flung themselves to the ground and, after a few moments of bewildered silence, pandemonium ensued. Clare began screaming, the Nigerian girls were moaning in pain, the detective was shouting, so too were other workers and residents of the refuge who came rushing out, bystanders began arriving offering help in the confusion, police walkie-talkies were blaring and first-aid was being vigorously applied as the panic and confusion continued. Only Irina Lockyer remained silent. Miraculously, neither the detective nor Clare were struck, both girls caught bullets but not, it transpired, in a way that threatened their lives. However, Irina was shot through the head and killed instantly. She lay on her back, her head resting one step lower than the rest of her, her eyes half-closed, her mouth half open and her blood flowing gently from her temple down the steps and on to the pavement. Beside her lay her bag from which a pair of knitting needles protruded. Death is no respecter of dignity. Visible for all to see were her olive green bloomers. Clare began to sob as she recounted the events and buried her head into Robbie's chest. He stroked her hair tenderly as the police car sped them away. She knew that the image of this dying old woman was one that she would retain to her dying day.

As they arrived at the police station, colleagues, eager to determine what had happened, mobbed the two officers. A kindly policewoman arranged for cups of tea. Eventually, after what seemed an interminable wait, a detective invited Clare into a briefing room to compose a witness statement. Robbie was also allowed in on condition he did no more than comfort his distraught wife. Clare recalled the events once more, having already given her version of them to police at the scene. The detective apologised for the repetition required but Clare understood and continued. When pressed, she was unable to say anything useful in her mind, about the car from which the gunfire had come, other than that it was dark in colour. She did not see the registration number nor knew of its make. She spoke about the mission to deliver the two Nigerian girls into a safer environment and then described the man she had questioned who had been snooping around the house two days previous. She said he was a white male aged around 45, tall, say six foot, dark brown hair, not unattractive but with no unusual features. Clare informed her inquisitor that the detective on the scene had recovered the CCTV footage from the DVD player of the person of whom she was speaking. The officer nodded that he had the disc, pressed a button on the DVD player and asked her to confirm that this was the man in question. Robbie nearly fell off his chair.

"Good God," he cried.

"Please sir, I must insist you stay quiet during this procedure."

"No, you don't understand. I know this man. It's my friend Steve Graham. I commute with him every day. I don't believe it. Steve Graham."

"And you'd never met this man before?" asked the detective, looking at Clare.

"I know the name from my husband but I'd never met him until the other day," she replied looking somewhat bemused.

Unfortunately for Steve, Robbie hadn't been on the train when he told the tale of how he had followed The Crone and as a result could offer no explanation for his appearance on the security camera footage. But he assured the detectives that Steve could never have murdered anyone.

The look of incredulity on Robbie's face when he saw Steve's picture was matched by that of Steve himself when he turned on his phone later that night. He had switched it off to abide by the rules of the hospital in which he was visiting one of his best friends and fellow journalist, Darren Simmons, who'd suffered a mild heart attack a few days earlier. He'd sneaked in a bottle of Aussie Merlot, purloined a couple of plastic glasses from the water cooler and the two hacks surreptitiously enjoyed the fruits of the Barossa Valley while reliving old tales of derring-do in the newsroom, slandering members of the Herald's management team and catching up on gossip particularly about members of the paper's cricket team for which Steve used to open and Darren to keep wicket. Steve had intended staying an hour but got drawn into an animated conversation about sledging in cricket. Darren had wanted umpires to put a stop to it, believing that using abuse and insults to unsettle a batsman was "not cricket". Steve argued that a ban would be difficult to enforce but that he believed it was reasonable to sledge so long as the sledger and sledgee could enjoy a drink afterwards. Easier said than done was Darren's argument and just because the practice threw up the occasional witticism, most of the time the exchanges were quite ugly and not conversant with harmonious sporting relations. Darren could not resist a smile, however, when Steve revived memories of how one particular fast bowler, after being hit for six, muttered something insulting about the batsman's wife, a standard sledging technique. Unfortunately, his abuse contained particular anatomical details of which only someone with an intimate knowledge of his wife could have been aware. The result was a fistfight such as had never been seen on a cricket pitch before or since. Steve then questioned whether harmonious relations were necessary since they could come at the expense of fierce rivalry. So the argument continued, introducing elements of philosophy and politics into the discussion which would have undoubtedly led to the meaning of life had not time been called by a nurse anxious for Darren not to excite himself too much given his condition.

Among the text messages on Steve's phone were several from his wife, friends and colleagues in the newsroom asking him to call straight away. He called Maria but the line was engaged, so he called the newsroom instead. His call was answered by the chief sub-editor, a colleague he knew well.

"Hi, it's Steve Graham. Has something happened? Has the Queen died?

"Ah Steve, there you are, where the hell are you?"

"I'm around, what's going on?"

"You're a wanted man."

"I know I'm a wanted man. Everybody wants me? They just won't leave me alone."

"Wanted for murder, mate."

Steve paused and body began to tremble at these words as the instinctive secretion of adrenaline into his bloodstream took immediate effect.

"Are you pissing me about, Brian?" he said with a good deal more fear and urgency in his voice.

"No, honestly mate, I don't know what you've been up to but the police wired us a picture of someone they want to question about a murder near Blackfriars and it looks an awfully lot like you."

"Is this a wind-up, Brian?" By now, Steve could feel the muscles tensing in his face.

"No, mate, honest. Some old woman was gunned down and a person that looks rather like you was seen hanging around the place where it happened."

"This place. It wouldn't be Belvedere Crescent, would it?"

"Let me see....yes, that's right, Belvedere Crescent."

"Oh my God," Steve exclaimed.

He repeated it. "Oh my God!"

"You'd better turn yourself in, mate. I've got the old bill's number here.

"I didn't do it, Brian, and you can quote me if you like. It's all a big misunderstanding and I'll clear it up as soon as I can."

He took down the number and immediately rang it. He explained everything to the duty clerk and was told that a police car would pick him up straight away. He had enough time to call Maria again on the landline and this time she answered. She was frantic with worry, asking him repeatedly where he was and what was going on. He didn't have time to explain it all to her and when he gave her the bare bones, she sounded utterly confused. Steve had to assure her repeatedly that it was all a misunderstanding and that he would clear up the confusion as soon as he could but that he was unlikely to see her tonight since it was already nearly midnight. When the police car arrived at a predetermined location, three armed policemen with flak jackets jumped out, read him his rights, handcuffed him and bundled him into the back of the car in a heavy-handed manner. The car was then driven off at speed, siren blaring.

"I always wanted to ride in a police car," ventured Steve, trying to make conversation. He was content in his own mind that matters would soon be resolved in his favour though the same could not be said of the car's other occupants.

"You know I was going to be a policeman once," he continued, "but I decided to finish primary school instead."

Without a word being spoken, the officer sitting next to Steve slapped him hard on the side of his face.

"Bit of a stand-up comedian are we, sir?" spoke the officer sitting in the passenger seat turning to face their prisoner.

“Like a bit of comedy do you in between murdering old, defenceless women?”

“I haven’t murdered anyone,” protested a somewhat chastened Steve, rubbing his cheek. “I’m a journalist, for Christ’s sake.”

At this, the three policemen burst into laughter in unison.

“What a comedian you are, sir,” voiced the one sitting next to him and gave him another, harder, slap.

Steve regretted his naïve non sequitur and decided that if he were to retain any measure of his looks it would be in his interest to button his lip for the rest of the journey before one of these monkeys fattened it.

Fortunately, the journey did not last long and Steve was hauled into an interview room. A middle-aged female officer, DCI Medlock, then conducted a short interview that began with the obvious question establishing his whereabouts at 6.45pm that day. In fact, Steve had just left work some 15 minutes before and, as he put it, “would not have had time to drive to Belvedere Crescent in a car I don’t own and shoot an old lady who I don’t know with a gun I don’t have.” Steve was then asked to explain why he had been caught on CCTV outside 19 Belvedere Crescent earlier that week.

“I was following this old lady as a bit of a joke,” he admitted, confident that he would soon be cleared but embarrassed by the puerility of his actions that day.

“You stalk old ladies for fun do you, Mr Graham?” said Medlock in the deadest of deadpan ways.

“I wasn’t stalking her, I was just following her.”

”Is it normal for you to follow old ladies, Mr Graham? Do you derive some sort of sexual pleasure from this pastime?”

”What?”

“Do old ladies turn you on, Mr Graham? Get you horny do they?”

Steve paused. “Only on Thursdays, Inspector, when the wind is blowing from the south-east.”

Now the inspector paused. “Following old ladies – a bit childish at least, don’t you think?”

“Childish? Not particularly.”

“Do you have children Mr Graham?”

“Yes, once a week in the back of my car actually. I lure them in with bars of chocolate – Mars bars to be precise, king-size but not deep-fried.”

DCI Medlock remained deadpan, looking Steve in the eye. Finally she relented.

“Alright Mr Graham, let’s start this again. Explain what happened.”

“Oooh, thank you, may I?

By the time Steve had explained everything to DCI Medlock, her tone mollified. Inwardly, she was even quite amused. Steve not only recalled the incident with the blue BMW and the hostile reaction he received on seeking directions, but from the back of his memory bank he mustered the fact that its registration number included his initials SG. The officer, pleased with this information, was positively apologetic, more so when she informed Steve that, as the hour was late and there was no one to formally check alibis both for the murder and for Steve’s pathetic pursuit, Steve was invited to remain in the cell overnight, no doubt, thought Steve, alongside all the drunks, prostitutes and ne’er do wells. He was not best pleased. As it turned out his fears were not justified. Before he was shown the way, however, a sudden thought struck him.

“You didn’t tell me if the old lady who was shot was the one I was following?”

“I can’t tell you that, Mr Graham.”

“Can’t tell me because it’s confidential?”

”No, because I don’t know who you were following?”

“She was grey-haired, around 80, cross between an academic and a bag lady?”

“Could be, but that could fit many old ladies.”

”Did she knit?”

11 RUTH

Ben closed his front door quietly and began walking to the station. He closed it quietly because Elizabeth was still sleeping; he began walking because someone had stolen his bike, again. Elizabeth wouldn't normally be asleep when he left for work. In fact, since she had to drive each day to the business premises where she worked as an architect, a half-hour journey, it was customary for her to leave before him. However, Ben was leaving early to try to discover which wretched soul would be desperate to steal a rust bucket that purported to be a bicycle, and he was leaving early to confirm the alibi of an equally wretched soul who'd managed to entangle himself in a murder case by following an old woman they called The Crone.

It was a beautiful autumn morning. It had been raining during the night but the clouds had parted enough to allow the sun to cast upon the roads and pavements a silvery sheen. He looked back momentarily at his home, a four-bedroom detached Edwardian townhouse in which he and Elizabeth had lived for more than a decade. Since his two sons had both graduated and left home, his wife and he had often talked about moving to a small apartment more insulated from the winters that seemed to be growing ever colder by the year. However, both would miss the garden and Ben loved nothing more than to sit out in it on a warm summer's evening enjoying glasses of wine with friends. Ben had become aware that his weekly intake of alcohol, while not large by his friends' standards, nevertheless exceeded government guidelines. It was an inconsistency in his otherwise healthy lifestyle that included daily exercise and a diet that nodded firmly in the direction of the Mediterranean with plenty of olive oil, fish, nuts, fruit and vegetables though with perhaps more red meat than the Latins were accustomed to consume. Elizabeth had been the inspiration for what for him had been a gradual brainwashing into eating more sensibly. Ben had been brought up on fish and chip suppers and Sunday roasts. The main argument in his family centred on how long the beef should be cooked.

He still relished the occasional crude assault on his taste buds by a side portion of brown-sauced chips or a fast-food burger but it was their infrequency as much as their flavour that made them taste special. It was that glass of wine after work with Elizabeth that became two then three, then seeing no point in leaving just a little in the bottle, that was at the root of the problem. So Ben attempted to reduce his wine consumption by disciplining himself to take it only with food. The upshot was that he began eating like there was no tomorrow. Instead, he convinced himself that the quality of life should be a factor in a healthy lifestyle and that happiness would negate any subconscious nervousness of the effects of over-drinking. And it was healthier than whisky perhaps. In other words, there was no problem. As he walked on, Ben noticed a neighbour.

"Morning Brian, how are you?"

"How am I? Is that a loaded question, Mr Obituary Man?"

Ben smiled. "You look pretty healthy to me, Brian. I'd give you at least six months."

"How generous. You're up early this morning, Ben. Somebody died?"

"No Brian. But if I had to get up every day at this time like you do it wouldn't be long before I died, I can tell you."

"Nah, you get used to it. How's Elizabeth?"

"In bed."

"Who with?"

"Now, now Brian, it's far too early for jokes like that."

"And the boys, both well?"

"Yes, Charles is doing his articles with a solicitor in London and James is working with a local newspaper in Kent."

"Following his Dad, eh? Do you see much of them?"

"Well, actually Brian, they come round all the time to give us money. Every time they have a bit of spare cash, round they come."

Brian smiled.

"You know only the other night while Elizabeth and I were in bed, I heard this noise from outside our door. I went down and there was a pile of banknotes that they'd left for us. It took me an hour to bring them all in."

"Bankrupting you are they?"

"Nearly."

Brian smiled again, lowered himself into his vehicle and waved before shutting the door. As Ben walked on it occurred to him that Brian was one of the few people he knew from his town who didn't commute. Commuting each day made for a somewhat odd relationship with the place. He spent more waking hours either in London or on a train than he did in his hometown. To a lesser extent the same was true of Elizabeth. As a result, their social circle was not as wide as it would have been had they not travelled to a different place each day. What's more, their sense of identity with their community was not as strong as it might otherwise have been and this was exacerbated by the fact of their children having both relocated to the capital. They often talked about moving away after their retirement but without specifying where. Elizabeth had often talked of a small cottage in the country where a goat would keep the grass down and chickens provide fresh eggs. Ben, however, couldn't bear the thought of being more than a couple of hundred yards from a cappuccino and loved the fact that he was within walking distance to whatever amenities he needed. The station, however, was not within walking distance on a daily basis and the need for a replacement bike was therefore a priority. But to satisfy his thirst for justice, he wanted to make an effort to discover the identity of the thief even though he knew in his heart of hearts that he was probably pursuing a lost cause. That instinct was confirmed when he arrived at the station's so-called security centre, situated on one of the main platforms. For in the midst of a bank of CCTV monitors, one appeared blank.

"Why is this one turned off?" Ben asked politely of one of the three officials on duty.

"It's not, it's just crap quality," came the reply from one with an apologetic smile.

"I see. I suppose you're going to tell me that this is the one that monitors the bike shed."

"Right first time, guv'nor. You've been here before."

"I have been here before but I was of the naïve opinion that the technology here might have improved."

"What, in this time of economic recession? You've gotta be kidding, mate."

"So no point in looking at the tape for yesterday then?"

"Well you might just see the man in the dark coal cellar looking for the black cat that isn't there."

Ben was not amused. As he made his way out, one of them asked him, "Aren't you the bloke who lost his shoe up on the rafters?"

Before the man could continue, Ben interrupted with "Good morning, gentlemen", which only provoked laughter and the remark "Maybe your bike's up there and all."

As Ben walked away he thought to himself that someone must have told these men about his shoe incident because they could never have seen it on the bloody CCTV.

As he proceeded on to the platform he noticed Hilary buried in a newspaper. When he called her name, her expression when she looked up was one of disbelief.

"Have you seen whose picture is on the front page?"

"Tell me about it," was Ben's rather resigned reply.

"I got a call early this morning from Steve. He'd spent the night in custody while they sorted out his alibi. I've got to go down to the station now to confirm his story about The Crone."

"I can't believe it," said Hilary with a look of resignation.

"I think it was your bright suggestion that someone should follow her."

"It was," said Hilary nodding her head. "It was definitely The Crone then?"

"Yep, she was the only old woman who worked there."

"The poor old thing," said Hilary. "But have you seen what they've been saying about Steve?"

Ben took hold of the paper, which, judging from what Steve had told him in his early morning call, must have been an early edition. Hilary pointed to the last sentence in the report.

"Police are not commenting on speculation that there might be a connection between Mr Graham's profession of obituary writer and the death of Mrs Lockyer."

Ben burst out with a cynical laugh.

"What do they think is going on? Is this reporter saying that Steve was murdering people to create material for his obits column? I ask you." He paused.

"Actually, that's not a bad idea, I must get a gun."

"Who would you shoot first, then?" asked Hilary, smiling.

"The bastard who stole my bike last night, that's who. That's why I was in that office. If the house where The Crone was shot had a CCTV camera like the ones in this station, Steve would be with us on the train now."

As the train began inching its way into the platform, Robbie came rushing up to the pair of them. Both were shocked when he told them of Clare's presence at the shooting. Robbie assured them that though she was initially traumatised, she was doing well and had gone to work this morning.

"Does Steve know that Clare was a witness?"

"He didn't and he was as surprised as you are when I rang him this morning. I wasn't expecting to get through to him but he seemed relatively chipper given the circumstances. I gather you're going to meet him, Ben."

"Yes, I'm going to formally extricate the little sod from a mess of his own making, or of Hilary's making?"

Hilary shot back a sarcastic smile. They all agreed on how disturbing the whole affair was and they couldn't imagine what the family of The Crone must be going through. This was very much in Steve's mind when Ben met him at the police station.

"Irina Lockyer. I'd never have put her as Irina Lockyer. I had her down as Gladys Higginbotham."

"Well either's better than The Crone," Ben replied to Steve's ruminations.

"The Crone seems a very cruel name now."

Amid the flurry of visiting family and friends, social workers, translators, probation officers, solicitors and others associated with the criminal justice system, Steve found a space on a table on which to complete his formalities. He then noticed a woman in the waiting room sobbing gently and dabbing her eyes with a tissue. She was in her late 50s, Steve estimated, rather conservatively dressed in a worsted suit and sensible shoes. He took pity on her and offered to fetch her a cup of tea. The woman appeared grateful and when she looked up to thank him was taken aback when she recognised him as the man in the photograph in the paper.

“It was you. You were there when my mother was killed.”

Steve was taken aback. “Your mother, you mean Irina Lockyer? No, no, no,” he exclaimed, seeing the fear in her eyes.

“I wasn’t there at all. I was identified as having been there a few days ago. It was all a misunderstanding.”

The woman’s face grew less taut. “Did you know my mother?”

“I didn’t know her except by sight. The truth is, sorry I don’t know your name...”

"Ruth, Ruth Lockyer."

"Pleased to meet you Ruth, I’m Steve Graham and I’m so sorry about your mother. It’s almost too shocking for words.”

Ruth’s expression softened to one of puzzlement. “You’re the man who writes the obituaries, aren’t you?”

“That’s right.”

"So you were saying, about my mother?”

"Yes, I knew your mother by sight, Ruth. She and I take the same train, um, er took the same train. Sorry.” Steve looked almost as mortified as her mother.

"That's alright."

"I remember having a brief conversation with her once about knitting."

"Really?"

"Yes indeed," Steve lied. "My mother was a great knitter and I've always had a bit of a thing about it to be honest and I could see that your mother was very keen."

Steve was making all of this up as he went along. If Ben had heard any of it, he'd have probably been sick. Steve continued. "I remember when I would wear these old tank tops and woollen jumpers at college that Mum had knitted for me, I'd get ribbed endlessly. Not ribbed as in knitting ribbed, you know what I mean." Ruth's expression did not change.

"But when the cold winters came, they'd be pillaging my wardrobe for these woollies."

"Yes, Mum certainly loved her knitting. The women in the refuge loved her for it too. Though there's a sad story behind it. So how come you became involved?"

"I happened to be walking down Belvedere Crescent and I came across your mother by chance and noticed her walking into No. 19. So out of sheer curiosity, being a nosy journalist, I was just looking for a nameplate or something. I had no idea I was being filmed. Then when this dreadful shooting took place later, they put two and two together and made four hundred and fifty two."

Ruth wiped away a tear.

"Naturally, I had no idea it was a refuge and I can quite understand why I was raising suspicions. But everything's been sorted now as far as I'm concerned and I can only hope, Ruth, that those who killed your mother will be brought to justice as soon as possible."

After a short pause while she blew her nose, Ruth turned once more to Steve.

"My mother would make a fascinating obituary for you, you know."

"Really?" uttered Steve, genuinely surprised.

"She escaped all sorts of family trauma to become a linguist and worked for the BBC. She once did some work for the foreign office on a trades union mission to eastern Europe where she came from originally, you know."

"Really? said Steve, genuinely even more surprised.

"I don't know too much about what she did, she never really spoke about it but that's typical of her generation I think. She was never one to blow her own trumpet."

At this point in the conversation Ben appeared, having completed his business in verifying Steve's particulars, and was ready to leave.

"Well in that case, Ruth, here's my card and perhaps you can get in touch with me when you're feeling up to it. We must do justice to your mother in death in the way she deserves."

Ruth agreed, Steve handed over his card and they thanked each other.

"I know how difficult this must be for you and I hope it all goes well," were Steve's final words. Ruth nodded and smiled as he joined Ben and headed out of the door.

"Who was that? asked Ben.

"Ruth Lockyer."

"What, The Crone's daughter?"

"Yup, the daughter of someone whose obit I might well be writing."

"Really. So, you did murder her like it said in the paper," joked Ben.

"Not funny, Benny. Not funny at all."

As Steve wandered into the Herald's large open-plan newsroom, he felt everyone's eyes turn in his direction. In fact, only a few did but enough to utter comments like "Ladykiller" and "Obit hunter". He batted them away with a rueful smile to those he respected, and with a "Fuck off" to those he didn't. His line manager, obituaries editor Harry Fearnley, a stern-looking ex-military man, ushered him into his glass-walled office to determine what had been going on. Steve had barely begun his account when the editor-in-chief's personal assistant who was under orders to inform Steve that her boss wanted to see him right away, spotted him and redirected him upstairs. Nervously, Steve knocked on the door. Frank Butters was a tall, no-nonsense editor whose physical presence was intimidating enough even for seasoned hacks. Butters looked up and pointed to a chair opposite and considerably lower than his desk. Realising the psychological implications of such an arrangement, Steve said he'd prefer to stand with the excuse that he'd been sitting all day and would risk Deep Vein Thrombosis if he sat any more. Beside the desk was a television tuned into Sky News. On it, Steve saw Clare Blake, Robbie's wife, being interviewed.

"Listen to this for a moment, Steve," said Butters.

Clare was explaining to her interviewer that the trafficking of women was now the world's most lucrative black market activity behind weapons and drugs. She said that thousands of poor women from all over the world were being smuggled into Britain only to be raped on a daily basis as prostitutes or enslaved as so-called domestic servants.

"If William Wilberforce were alive today he would be ashamed. The slave trade that he helped abolish was now happening again but in secret. Yet what is the government doing to combat it? Nothing," she said with a confidence borne of conviction and media coaching. She

went on to assert that few convictions had been secured and that the police seemed more interested in finding girls like the ones who were injured in the shooting because they were illegal immigrants rather than victims of organised crime. She further maintained that the government should be releasing more funds for shelters for trafficked women. Had there been more of these desperately needed places, she argued, her organisation, the Daisy Project, would not have found it necessary to be using this temporary address for a refuge and, by implication, the shooting would not have taken place. Butters turned off the TV.

"So, Steve. First of all, I'd like your explanation as to why one of my journalists is splashed on the front pages of several newspapers. I like my employees to report the news, not make it."

Steve had predicted the question and had prepared his defence, a watered-down version of the truth. "I was as shocked as you were, Frank," he insisted. "Several days before, I happened to notice the old woman, the one who was shot, walking down the street. She travelled on the same train as me and I was just being nosey and wanted to know where she worked."

"You knew the woman?"

"I knew who she was, but I didn't know her. I think I spoke to her once. But, coincidentally, I also know the husband of the woman you just saw speaking on the TV."

"Really?" Butters paused. "So you weren't stalking this old lady?"

Steve blew out his cheeks in a disapproving way. "Of course not, why would I do that?" he said, having decided that to tell the precise truth would have been too embarrassing. "I'm not some kind of sick pervert, Frank."

"Glad to hear it. You can see," continued the editor who was by now pacing around his office, "how the story has become a political issue. It takes the killing of someone like an old woman who was a good servant of the community and so on to capture the public imagination. Now the government is under attack for not taking this trafficking issue seriously. Backbenchers are even coming out against the prime minister. There's a lot of mileage in this one. Can you arrange for this Blake woman to give us a full-page profile? I want to know personal stories, ones that will tug at people's heart strings."

Steve took on the air of self-satisfaction. "I can't see that as being a problem, Frank."

"And what about this old woman? Have you got anything interesting to say about her that we haven't heard already?"

"What have you heard? I haven't been able to see or read much in the past few hours."

"Just that she was helping out at the refuge on a voluntary basis. Is there a particular reason why she did that, for example?"

"I know no more than you do on that," Steve answered. "I'm told though that she might make an interesting obituary."

"Who told you?"

"I met her daughter at the police station. She told me that her mother had an interesting life, was a keen knitter and all round good egg. As you can imagine, she's deeply traumatised at the moment, so I've told her to contact me when she's feeling better. I think she'll co-operate with my obit."

Frank Butters turned to Steve with a face that looked as if he was about to spit. "Well you can keep the bloody knitting for your obituary. If you come across anything interesting, let me know, do you hear?"

"Of course, Frank. You do know that I might have stumbled upon the prime suspects?"

"What do you mean?" The editor's expression was now decidedly quizzical.

“I asked these characters for directions. They were parked a few yards away in a car and more or less told me where to go in what sounded to me like east European accents.”

"Well you’d better go and see the crime desk guys and tell them what you know and speak to the features people and sort out this profile. And stay out of the bloody news, alright? This “obit hunter” business is bloody embarrassing.” Butters all but banged his fist on his desk.

"Alright, Frank.”

“And seeing those guys makes you a potential trial witness, so watch your back. And after you’ve talked to the crime guys, go home and get some rest. You look a mess.”

"OK, thanks Frank.”

Steve thought, as he left the office, that Frank Butters was a pussycat compared to the reception he would have to face from Maria.

12 ANTHONY

Steve didn't make the train the following day. It was as well he didn't because the probability was that he might have entangled himself in a confrontation in more ways than one. As Ben installed himself by the window, for once ahead in the rush to be seated, an obese man sat himself down in the middle seat opposite him, sweating profusely from the effort merely of boarding the train. As Ben later described him, he wasn't obese merely in the clinical sense of possessing a Body Mass Index of more than 30. "He's the size of a pregnant blue whale!" His torso spread both sideways and forwards giving the impression he was slumped into his seat when, in fact, he was sitting as normally as he could. Robbie who took up the place beside him had to rotate his sitting position 90 degrees in order to find a position for his feet, in the aisle. This made conversation difficult since he was now facing away from his companions, so he took out a crossword and began reading the clues. A woman sat on the other aisle seat leaving the only available place opposite the obese man.

As grotesque as he found the sight of obese people, Ben was not entirely lacking in sympathy for them. He didn't know, for example, if this man had been stuffed full of junk food by his parents from an early age or if he suffered from a thyroid complaint or had made efforts to lose weight, though if this was the case he had been spectacularly unsuccessful. Ben had often reflected that had he not been blessed with a high metabolic rate, his voracious appetite might have placed him firmly in the obese bracket. This particular man was well dressed in a three-piece suit, less Paul Smith, more Cyril. Ben thought to himself that his tailor would have taken his measurements in metres rather than centimetres, and his order alone would have kept a Chinese sweatshop in business for weeks. The man augmented his repugnant image by the heaviness of his breathing, like a pot-bellied pig sleeping off a hangover.

All was going well until Hilary arrived on the scene. Anxious to talk to

Ben and Robbie about The Crone shooting, she welcomed the sight of the blue-coloured textile that signified a vacant seat opposite the Behemoth, thought twice about the inevitable squeeze but decided nevertheless to proceed seeing as she was a slip of a girl, little over 5 foot 3. Once installed, Hilary felt rather uncomfortable, not just because she had almost no leg room and was practically playing Ride A Cock Horse with Mammoth Man, but she was wearing a short skirt which was forced to go even shorter given the raised position her legs were forced to adopt. Ben exacerbated her discomfort by remarking on what a fine pair of pins she possessed, and it was partly to compensate for his lack of tact that he made a suggestion that he soon came to regret. He offered to swap seats with Hilary and before she could argue over the utter impracticality of such a notion, hoisted her up from her seat and somehow managed to swing his body around into the vacant space and placing Hilary on to his lap, much to her ever-increasing embarrassment which she expressed audibly with a series of shrieks. Ben then swung his legs on top of those of the obese man and deposited Hilary at the same time in the window seat. In so doing, he managed to dig one of his heels directly into the genitalia of the large man in question causing a piercing cry of pain. The man was in agony, and as his muscles tightened instinctively he trapped Ben's foot between his legs. The pair resembled a drawing from the Kama Sutra with the rolls of fat around the man's torso sucking in Ben's leg like human quicksand. Ben's attempts to free himself from this quagmire of flab caused him to press his knee heavily against the man's gonads releasing further agonising yells. This was a most vicious of vicious circles. In the meantime, Robbie and the other woman were unable to stifle their laughter. Other commuters standing in the aisle and who had been distracted by the commotion were initially alarmed, then highly amused. Even Hilary was now laughing, and the more Ben struggled to free himself and the more the obese man suffered physically and very audibly as a result, the more hilarious it became.

Eventually, Ben managed to break free and decided wisely that he would stand for the rest of the journey. Had the obese man seen the funny side of the whole business that had lasted but a couple of minutes, the matter would have ended there. Unfortunately, he didn't and lambasted Ben for the absurdity of the manoeuvre he had performed. Though this was not an unreasonable point of view, the manner in which he expressed it changed the atmosphere. Ben wanted to say to him, "Look mate, you've only paid for one seat but you're taking up two. The problem is with you not with us." He also imagined the kind of reaction the man's attitude would have provoked had Steve been present. It would doubtless have involved threats of implements being thrust into various orifices. However, Ben decided he'd caused enough trouble and opted to remain silent, offering only a mild look of disdain. It was left to the mild-mannered Robbie to break the ensuing silence.

"Help me with this clue, guys. Daft as brat, anagram, 3, 7."

When Ben arrived in the office, instead of the Abba singsongs, The Stick's latest trauma or golf games that were the normal activities first thing in the morning, an air of seriousness pervaded the atmosphere. The two men were at their desks working away as if the headmaster had been in and read the riot act. The reason soon became apparent. Anthony was having to draft a statement for the press office over a report in one of the national papers that the BBC had been preparing an obituary of a drug addicted, alcoholic pop star. Several celebrity gossip websites were also running the story.

"They just don't get it, do they," moaned Anthony. He continued:

"Just because we prepare an obit of someone doesn't mean we're hoping that they die. Well, not officially anyway. Wouldn't worry me if the old cow snuffed it tomorrow. Never could stand her music, but that's not the point."

To Ben, this was something of a rite of passage for all obituary writers. He'd had the same experience with the football manager Brian Clough for whom he'd pre-prepared an obit years before he died when he heard that the legendary footballer and manager had developed a drink problem. Someone found out and it appeared in a newspaper with no regard as to the feelings of Mr Clough himself should he have found out about it. Similarly a former colleague had prepared an obit of Britney Spears, which was produced because at the time her increasingly bizarre behaviour indicated that she was an accident waiting to happen. Again, it found itself in a newspaper even though every other broadsheet was undoubtedly making the same preparations. Thankfully for Ms Spears, she came through her ordeal.

"The tabloids would be the first to complain if your woman did die and we hadn't prepared anything," said Ben.

"They probably wouldn't even notice, they'd be too busy over-emoting," replied Anthony before boo-hooing in an exaggerated, thespian manner.

"How did they find out?" Ben asked.

"I was in the bar talking to Dougie Brown. He must have had some of his journalist mates with him because I recognised some of my phrasing in the report. I should claim bloody royalties."

"Careless talk...."

"Yes, I know, ... Anybody'd think we killed her."

"Well if it's any consolation this has happened to me twice. I remember the legendary gossip columnist Nigel Dempster ringing me up after someone in his team had discovered we'd prepared an obit on some celebrity or other. I explained to him in great detail that any serious media outlet prepares obits in advance of people who are old, ill or vulnerable. I noted that his paper, The Daily Mail, didn't include obituaries. That's probably why he took absolutely no notice and published anyway despite my trying to persuade him that there wasn't a story."

Ben rose from his desk and walked to the water-cooler and helped himself to a cup.

"Anyway, preparation works. When Amy Winehouse died, who had an obit ready?" enthused Anthony.

"Yes, and Paula Yates too," echoed Ben.

"I remember the obituary of Nico, the singer with the 1970s group The Velvet Underground? She died in a road accident. One paper wrote, 'She gave up heroin for bicycling which turned out to be the more dangerous amusement.'"

"Love it," said Anthony.

"So what are you saying to the publicity people?"

Anthony peered at his computer screen and read a sentence from his statement, *"We do not wish any misfortune to happen and hope that she lives to be a hundred and more, but in the event of her death given her well-documented health problems, we need to be prepared."*

"That should do it."

At these words, The Stick made her entrance looking tense and somewhat dishevelled. As she began removing her coat she offered her excuse for her tardiness.

"Sorry I'm late, my boyfriend stole my boat."

Her three colleagues looked at each other and smiled mischievously knowing first that she was serious and secondly that if they asked her to explain they'd never get any work done.

"That's alright Sticky, it happens to us all," said Ben.

Ben informed The Stick about Anthony's unfortunate indiscretion and why he felt the need to supply a short explanation. Ben said that he lost no sleep over such trivial stories but that they occasionally received complaints from viewers that required more thoughtful responses. For example, however balanced one might try to be when assessing the careers of controversial leaders such as the former Serbian leader Slobadan Milosevic and the PLO head Yasser Arafat, for example, there would always be supporters who will dispute anything they don't like in the obituary. In the case of Milosevic, for example, there were complaints that mention was made of accusations that he fanned the flames of Serbian nationalism to consolidate his own power and that he was responsible for ethnic cleansing and subsequent war crimes. The BBC, Ben argued, didn't extradite Milosevic to the International Criminal Court in The Hague where these charges and others were laid against him. However, Ben argued, sometimes one has to trust in the opinion of the foreign correspondents who follow these political figures closely. For example, when Carla Wilson had described Arafat's PLO as an organisation riddled with corruption and cronyism, he had to go with it regardless of what others might believe. Ben continued that the danger of trying to be balanced is that you can end up defending the indefensible. However, saying unkind things about less controversial figures on the day their deaths were announced could appear churlish. That, he noted with some degree of envy, remains one of the main differences between a broadcast obituary on the TV news and news website, and one published in the newspaper or the newspaper website that can be more considered.

"De mortis nil nisi bonum," said The Stick.

"And the same to you," replied Anthony.

"De mortis nil nisi bonum," repeated The Stick unabashed. "Of the dead speak only good. What happened to that convention?"

"Well it more or less holds in broadcast terms apart from the Hitlers and Pol Pots of this world, but in general that went the way of deference to the royal family and the breakdown of many other conventions in the media."

“Actually,” interjected Anthony, “That convention of which The Stick so eloquently spake was a bit of a fashion.” He opened a desk drawer and began rummaging through a pile of papers within it.

“Somewhere in here I’ve got a couple of examples in history of where not particularly nice things were said about newly departed notables. I know they’re here somewhere.”

“Your library needs a major reorganisation, Anthony,” declared The Stick.

“Are you offering?” he countered.

“No I am not. I wouldn’t touch your library with yours.”

”Well you’d be missing out,” cried Anthony as he came upon the file for which he’d been searching. He extracted two pieces of A4 paper on both of which were written a quotation.

“This is one from The Gentleman’s Magazine of 1851 about the Duke of Newcastle.”

Anthony began reading with a pronounced relish in his delivery.

“The Duke of Newcastle. On various occasions he laid himself open to the bitterest assaults of popular indignation. Impressed with the ideas of rigid and extreme Conservatism, the Duke was violently opposed to all the constitutional changes that have marked the history of the last quarter of a century; whether they concerned the claims of the Protestant dissenters, Catholic emancipation or parliamentary reform. The late Duke found it necessary to fortify his mansion at Clumber and the windows of his town house in Portman Square were broken by the

London rabble."

The Stick smiled and agreed with Ben that there was something timeless about those words.

"And here's another one from the same era, from 1830 on King George IV. Get a load of this. *'The late King acquired if not an appetite for wasting money, an habit of prodigality, the most reckless, unceasing and unbounded. Nor has the country ceased to feel to this hour the effects of an indifference to the sufferings of others little creditable in him who so frequently aggravated or produced them. King George IV had many generations of intimates with whom he led a course of life the character of which rose little higher than that of animal indulgence.'"*

"We've gone backwards," suggested The Stick. "I'm not sure a broadsheet today would be that castigating about royalty."

"No, we leave that to Twitter and the other social networks," said Ben.

"So you see," said Anthony, "the Latin phrase you quoted about not speaking ill of the dead is something that comes in and out of fashion."

"I've seen fashions come and go in the 20 or so years I've been doing this job," said Ben.

He explained that one of the first tasks he had to complete was to tone down the Queen Mother's obituary since the consensus was that it was too gushing and sounded like it had been written in the 1950s. In particular, there were references to her "tirelessly" touring the East End of London after the Blitz so that she could, as she herself put it, "look the East End in the face". While it was felt that she undoubtedly helped raise morale and that she undoubtedly did work hard, she could at least go home to the Palace at night rather than have to live with her home in ruins.

"Obituaries are just like any other type of news. Fashions and styles change," added Anthony. Ben took up the thread. "I remember when I first started we always had to end with a still image of whoever's obit we were making. That seemed to be a convention. I got rid of that. I sometimes end with a still today though it has to be an excellent one, one nicely shot that will live show the subject off in a good light as with Mario Testino's pictures of Diana."

"Is that what you did in her obit, showed her off in a good light?" asked The Stick"

"Well, that's a good case in point," answered Ben who began walking about the room with an air of headmasterly authority, as if practising for the chair in media studies to which he aspired for his retirement.

"Like with the Queen Mum, if we'd written nasty things about her then there'd have been a real backlash. It wouldn't have been the right time or the place. It's just that we didn't gush. In fact, I remember in one line we mentioned that Diana manipulated the media as indeed they manipulated her. To some extent, Diana broke the rules about airing dirty linen in public. I've got to be careful here because Anthony is going to pull something else out of his desk again and tell me that they always did it."

"Afraid not," Anthony interjected.

" So her obit was far more engaging because there was lots of human drama, not just foreign tours and opening fetes. Princess Margaret was the same. From a journalistic point of view, it's much more interesting having someone who nearly renounced her position in the royal family, married, separated, had affairs with toy boys, and was a bit of a pain in the arse. You might not always like the people you write about but if they're a bit naughty, or go against the grain or convention, then they're more fun to do."

"So you'd mention all the Duke of Edinburgh's gaffes then?" asked The Stick.

"Well when I first came here, it was felt to be tactless and inappropriate. But not long afterwards there came the realisation that his gaffes say something about the man and you can make your own judgements about him. Weaknesses, eccentricities, gaffes, these are all human qualities that make a story. People like a good story, I've told you that many times, Stick. And Margaret Thatcher's death with all the vitriol it produced from those who hated her shows me that criticism is part of the deal with obits. Everything today is in yer face. And the better the story, the better the obit, as long as, in our case, you've got some good video or audio to go with it. Talking of audio, you're a bit quiet today, Keith. Having trouble off the tee are you?"

There was no answer. Best leave him. The Stick carried on with what she was doing before Ben's entrance. She was sitting on the floor beside a tape player going through some rushes of Carla Wilson shot only a few days ago of her walking down a suburban street on a shoot for her gang report and performing a piece to camera about a spate of burglaries. Suddenly The Stick began to chortle. Having just finished filming the final take, the cameraman's phone began ringing. He answered it while forgetting to turn off the camera so that above the sight of cars driving to and fro was a disembodied one-sided conversation.

"Hey guys, come and listen to this," shouted The Stick, a broad smile on her face.

The others ambled over to see what was amusing her. The Stick wound back the tape to where the cameraman answered his call.

"Hello love, what's up? Not at school?"

"The spider? Ah yes."

"I know I said I'd move it, love, but I couldn't find it."

"I think I'd have seen it if it was as big as a house, darling"

"We don't have tarantulas in this country, love."

Ben and Anthony began to chuckle. Even Keith was showing an interest.

"Well it might have come on a boat like in that film but it's not very likely, darling."

"There's a frog in the kitchen as well?"

"Next to the spider? By the door?"

"I can't come back now, love, I'm working. Can't Mum sort it?"

"She's in the corner what?"

"Crying?"

"Don't worry darling, maybe the frog will eat the spider."

"No, I wasn't being funny, love."

"It's moving?"

"What, the spider or the frog?"

The three in the office were by now howling.

"Is that Mum screaming?"

"No, don't darling, the police will only come in an emergency, love."

"I know it looks like an emergency to you, love, but I think the police will be very cross if you call them."

"No, Mum doesn't need an ambulance."

"Hey, wait a minute," cried Keith staring at the monitor in a sudden state of animation. "I don't believe it."

"Surely you don't think an ambulance is appropriate, Keith," asked Ben.

"Rewind the tape a bit, Stick."

The Stick complied.

"No, no, wind it back, a bit more. There." Keith was pointing animatedly at the screen at a blue BMW car that had stopped near to the camera.

"That's my car. You remember I told you the other day that my car was stolen. That's my car!"

"Are you sure?" asked Ben.

"I'm certain."

The Stick stopped the tape at the point at which the front of the car filled half the screen.

"I thought your registration was KB1, Keith."

"Ha-ha Anthony. It's not my registration. Those are false plates and before you ask me how I know, I can tell you. First it's my make and colour, but it's the missing badge and the dent next to it. See them?"

"That could happen to any car "

"Yes but Ben, this is how I know. Whoever stole the badge dented the bodywork and I tried to repaint it, you know touch it up. But I used the wrong shade of paint and made a bit of a mess of it. See it? I can tell you, 100 per cent, that's my car."

"Yes, I can see your handiwork in all its glory," mused Anthony.

"I see your painting skills are much like those of your golf," added Ben.

The Stick pressed the play button. The car door opened as the frog began jumping towards the spider. Suddenly there was a general intake of breath as into the car stepped a familiar figure. The door closed and off it drove as the spider appeared to be moving too. Distant screams were now audible.

"Good God," exclaimed Ben. "It's her fiancé."

"No doubt about it, that's him," echoed The Stick turning towards Ben.

"That's terrible," added Anthony still looking at the screen. "The frog's going to eat the spider too. Spool it on Stick and you might find your boat."

Ben ignored Anthony. "If you're right, Keith, then why would whatshisname be getting into a stolen car?"

Keith nodded and immediately called his local police station and explained what they had just witnessed. On request, he gave the officer on duty what he believed was the false registration visible, SG12 PBC.

The Stick stared at the monitor with a piteous look. "And he's so gorgeous."

13 MARIA

Steve's absence from the train that morning was due to a sincere feeling of remorse, a large helping of humility and a promise that he would take Naomi and William to school every morning for a week. Maria had been frantic with worry when Steve hadn't appeared the day before The Crone's murder. Steve had assured her that he was having problems with a new phone and had since rectified the problem but that he had sent her a text reminding her that he was staying over in Suffolk where he had been interviewing friends of an obit subject. Indeed Steve had sent a text even though he knew his wife never checked her phone messages in the evenings. However, Maria did not recall ever having been made aware of her husband's planned overnight sojourn, neither, as she made clear in vociferous terms, had anyone else in his office. There developed a multi-stranded row in which Steve explained that his editor gave him free rein to interview people as and when he saw fit as long as he kept within certain budget restraints and held to his obituary deadlines, no pun intended. Consequently, he did not have to inform him of everything he was doing on a day-to-day basis. As to Maria's suggestion that he could phone these people up instead of interviewing them face-to-face, thereby enabling him to spend more time with his family, Steve launched into a fully-fledged defence of the practice emphasising the detail and colour that he derived from contact meetings which was what made the difference between a good and a very good obituary. What's more, he would often film clips of his interviewees for subsequent inclusion on the website. Maria was somewhat frustrated by the direction the argument had taken and felt Steve had in a sense blinded her with science. She was right.

But Maria's anger and frustration over this absence was nothing compared to that unleashed at his no-show over the following day's events. The couple were in the kitchen. Steve couldn't help thinking that he'd read years ago that wives are more likely to murder their husbands in the kitchen than in any other room in the house. However, it did not seem to him a timely idea to suggest they repair to the lounge. With her dark eyes wide and glaring, Maria let rip.

"How do you think I feel when practically every man and his dog ring me up to tell me that your picture is in the paper to do with the murder of an 80-year-old woman? How do you think I felt when the police ask where you are and I don't have a clue? How do you think I felt when my own parents ring me up and I don't have any idea as to what you were doing and where you were? And the same goes for your parents too." She paused to take a breath all the while glaring at Steve whose expression was decidedly hangdog. "And the looks I got when I took the kids to school! I felt like a criminal myself and yet I couldn't give an explanation, an excuse, nothing, because I hadn't heard a word from you."

Steve was on very shaky ground and he knew it. Though he responded to this onslaught with the excuse that he had tried several times to get through to her but in vain, the truth of the matter was that Maria and the kids had not been in the forefront of his mind over the past 48 hours. He had to admit that he had been caught up in a whirlwind and had, as a result, been entirely self-absorbed. He related in some detail the events that had occurred in an attempt to calm the waters and that he'd been forbidden to use his phone at the police station. He even came clean over what he was doing following the old lady though he referred to her as Irina Lockyer rather than The Crone. Maria was coruscating in her accusations of the childishness of his behaviour. She was right, again.

"God only knows what would have happened if you'd been outside that house on the day of the shooting," Maria cried.

Steve's body language was submissive. He took the point. As Maria began to sob, Steve felt the inevitable sense of guilt and sympathy for his wife for whom he had not been the person she had hoped for, the fully committed family man, always attentive to her needs in return for the sacrifices that she had made, albeit willingly, to devote herself to bringing up her family in the best Christian tradition. At the same time, he was all too aware of how divergent their paths through life were becoming. It wasn't just the religion, but somehow their interests had changed. He resented that she regarded him as professionally frustrated and failing to achieve his true potential when he certainly didn't feel so. The corollary, that his behaviour towards her and the family reflected this lack of fulfilment was even more galling. He resented her lack of interest in his work. He would have loved to discuss the subjects he had come across, the idiosyncrasies, the achievements and failures, the love, the passions, but he reserved that for people like Ben and Hilary. Why couldn't she be more like Hilary was a thought that had crossed his mind more than once. He could also enthuse about such matters with his parents but since they lived in the north the opportunities for such discussions were restricted to telephone conversations and to monthly visits. Steve believed that Maria had turned inward, devoting too much time to the children and not enough to him. Whatever the rights and wrongs of each other's arguments, there were clear symptoms of a marriage gone stale and in which the circles of interest were becoming less and less concentric.

Relations with Maria's parents were deteriorating too. They were a close family who saw a lot of each other since they lived less than two miles away and shared many of the social activities centred on the local Catholic Church. Maria was always helping her mother with bring and buy sales and fund raising for charitable projects in the developing world. There would be coffee mornings with the priest, and wine and cheese evenings with other parishioners. Steve had withdrawn from all of the activities he once embraced wholeheartedly and had been forced to justify his new atheist stance with Maria's father Gino in particular. The pair would argue, sometimes quite emotionally over matters of doctrine and the role of the Church in society.

"You betray God," Gino had told him. "God can forgive but you, Steve, without faith you will be lost."

It seemed to Steve, and he argued it strongly, that he seemed far more tolerant of Maria's beliefs than she or her family were of his. It was the seeming arrogance of this and of many religious people generally towards those non-believers like himself that Steve objected to most. He knew; he used to be like that. On the other hand, as a convert, albeit to atheism, Steve's criticisms were aimed most forcefully towards the minutiae of doctrine and the practices of Catholic religious observance that Maria's family regarded as much cultural as religious. This stridency irritated Gino in particular especially when the question of the sexual abuse by Catholic priests the world over and the hypocrisy of the Church's stand on homosexuality and priesthood celibacy made his arguments more difficult to defend to someone in iconoclastic mood.

"You cannot judge a religion based on the actions of a few dirty old men," he would argue. Gino, who doted on William and Naomi, had also become aware that Steve and his daughter had begun restricting the Church activities of his grandchildren. "Why you not let them go to Sunday School no more," he once exclaimed, exhibiting much frustration. This had been a negotiated compromise between man and wife but Gino felt Steve had imposed himself too much upon his daughter's beliefs, as to him religion was all or nothing. Their mutual antipathy had been simmering for months.

However, on the first day of Steve's contrition, Maria benefited not only from a lie-in but also a concession that Steve would conduct telephone interviews henceforth for obit subjects that would normally involve overnight stays. He wasn't happy about it but he kept his misgivings to himself. At least there was relative calm. Packed lunches had to be made, lost exercise books and pens had to be found, hair had to be brushed. There were complaints that Daddy doesn't do it properly the way Mummy does, but in general, both Naomi and William were always thrilled when Daddy took them to school. It was a sunny autumn day, the russets of the trees were in full range and glory and Steve decided, against a backdrop of childish objection, that the three would walk the three-quarter mile to school rather than take the car.

"Mummy never makes us walk," protested William. "The walk will do you good," came his father's response. Once en route, the complaining turned to mirth as the three gambolled hand in hand down the leafy suburban lanes. "Daddy, Patricia doesn't have to play football in games, can you ask Mr Brown if I can miss it too?" asked Naomi plaintively.

"I'm sure that Patricia had a good reason why she couldn't play and it would do you the world of good to join in."

Naomi was unimpressed. "Besides, how are you going to become Grimsby Girls' leading striker if you don't play football in school."

Yet Naomi and William laughed hysterically when William enacted an impression of Mr Brown the games master with his pronounced lisp. Steve was about to suggest that it was wrong to mock the afflicted, but decided that a lisp was not a real affliction and that he would have done exactly the same thing at their age. So he joined in the laughter too. In the end, the three of them spent the rest of the journey talking with a lisp. When Naomi spotted Mr Brown entering the main gate, she and William dissolved into more laughter. By the time Steve had kissed his children goodbye and watched each of them dash to be with one of their friends, he realised, as if he didn't know already deep down, that he was in danger of missing out on the most important aspect of his life through his imbalance towards work. He was musing on the subject as he walked back home. As he approached his house he noticed Gino's van parked beside it.

Gino was a short, squat Italian man who had emigrated from southern Italy in his teens along with his family. He had trained as a butcher, and had the stereotypical features associated with that profession in the form of ruddy cheeks, and muscular biceps and forearms fashioned from many decades of humping large carcasses. Gino had used his knowledge of meat – the best cuts, the optimum way to hang it and indeed the best way to cook and serve it – to develop a restaurant business. He now owned three Italian restaurants, all called Gino's, that were a step up from the bog standard pizza and pasta joints. His clientele was solidly middle-class and his subsequent progression into the wine importing business saw him mixing in ever more affluent circles. He was on the boards of three charities associated with Italy and he was well connected in his local church organisation. His social status within his small community was something of which he was most proud and anything that threatened to affect it adversely he took very seriously. When the picture of his son-in-law appeared in the national newspapers in connection with the murder of an old lady, Gino was deeply embarrassed. When he saw the distress on the face of his daughter when she confessed that she hadn't known his whereabouts for two days, Gino was livid. No matter how high fallutin the company he might sometimes keep, Gino was as down-to-earth as they come. The very idea that his daughter may be being mistreated in any way was like a blade to his heart. Steve knew that, as he pushed his key into his front door, he might be in for a rough ride.

The welcome Gino gave Steve was nothing more than cordial. In his heavily accented English he questioned him as they stood in the hallway as to the goings-on over the past few days. Maria tried to defend her husband by explaining matters in the exact way that Steve had done the previous night.

"Don't worry, Papa, Steve has explained everything to me."

Steve was quite glad to let Maria do the talking. It became clear to him though that Gino was sceptical of the account he was hearing merely because he continued staring at Steve throughout. Steve, in turn, never one to duck a challenge, stared straight back in the manner of a boxer at the start of a fight, as if daring Gino to dispute anything. Then he thought it appropriate to put his arm around Maria in a physical show of support and humility. Eventually, the conversation reverted to small talk. Steve inquired of Gino the state of his restaurant business but the answers he received were cursory. Gino was not yet done. To lighten the mood, Steve then related the fun he'd had with Naomi and William over Mr Brown's lisp and there were smiles all round. Eventually Gino had to leave and Steve accompanied him out to his van parked in the drive. The driver's side was not in view of the house and as Steve was about to say goodbye, Gino grabbed him forcefully by the lapel and said in a voice so heavy with gravitas that had it been a joint of meat it could have taken a hundred butchers to carry it,

"You mess with my daughter, Steve, and you gonna finda yourself ona my chopping block, understand?"

"You threatening me, Gino?"

"You can put it thata way, you can put it any way you fucking like, but justa remember what I justa tell you."

Steve was not only shocked by what his father-in-law had to say, but also because it was the first time he had heard Gino swear. It was a side of his father-in-law that he suspected was reserved for his workmates. Gino slid the door shut, continued to stare at his son-in-law and then pointed at him in a way that said, "Remember what I'm telling you." Steve wasn't sure whether to laugh or cry. He watched as Gino's van pulled away and wondered what on earth he'd got himself into. Why couldn't he just be the good family man, like Ben probably was? Thinking of Ben reminded him that he needed to catch the train. He looked at his watch and realised he needed to get going. He decided it was best to keep Gino's remarks to himself, so he kissed Maria goodbye, grabbed his car keys and headed towards the station.

14 TARAS

Steve ambled slowly down the avenue looking out for the number that signified where Ruth Lockyer lived or Chez Crone as he referred to it to his train colleagues. The road was lined on both sides with copper beech trees and the 1930s houses all boasted neatly-tended gardens that suggested to Steve either that each owner was proud enough not to want to let the neighbourhood down or was keeping up with Mr and Mrs Jones from number 42. When he arrived at Ruth's house, he was struck by the sight of the Virginia creeper spread around the front door at its most brilliant crimson and set off by a colourful mix of fading red and yellow roses, mauve potentilla and French lavender. It was quintessential British suburbia at its best. When Ruth answered the doorbell, Steve asked by way of small talk whether it was she that was responsible for the wonderful display of colour.

"I have to admit that it was my mother who had the green fingers in our family. I have trouble keeping indoor plants alive. How about you?"

"Yes, things around me tend to die too. Occupational hazard I guess." Steve smiled, realised a potential faux pas and quickly moved on.

"Did your mother live here long?"

"No, only a few years. I joined her here when she began finding it difficult to care for herself."

Inside, the house was quaint, full of dust, run-down and old-fashioned, a typical house of an academic, thought Steve, with overloaded, sagging bookcases. The carpets were threadbare and the place was furnished with the kind of heavy mahogany furniture fashionable in the 1970s. On the wall were family photographs, mostly black and white, many clearly dating many decades. A grandfather clock ticked noisily in the corner.

"Can I get you tea or coffee?"

"Tea please."

What Steve really wanted was a skinny cappuccino with a sprinkling of cinnamon but even if he had suggested this as a joke he doubted if Ruth would have found it funny. When the tea arrived, it came in a pot with a strainer and poured into bone-china floral cups riddled with hairline cracks. The small talk began over the coming to terms with the death of Irina. Ruth still had trouble reconciling the events of the previous week.

"I'd become used to the idea that my mother hadn't long to live. She was old and her health was failing. But to go in the way she did, at her age, I just can't believe it could have happened that way."

After a brief discussion over the tea and shortbread biscuits the pair finally got down to business, Steve setting his digital recorder on the table next to Ruth.

"Where do you want to begin?" began Ruth.

"Begin at the beginning and go on to the end and then stop," replied Steve.

"The Adventures of Irina in Wonderland," Ruth responded.

"How did your mother get the name Irina for a start?"

That question prompted something of a history lesson. It transpired that Irina was born in what is now the western part of Ukraine where she lived until she was 11 before coming to England. Her father, Ruth's grandfather, a man called Ostap Shevchenko, had come from a long line of farmers and was born at the turn of the 19th century when the region he came from, Galicia, was part of the Austro-Hungarian Empire. As a child, Ostap knew almost nothing but war. His country was fought over by Poles, Germans, Austrians and various Russian and Ukrainian factions. He and his family were caught in the middle but somehow they managed to survive. Ostap had a gift for drawing and painting and by the age of 20 had determined, against his parents' wishes, to leave farming and become an artist. By this time, he saw his region divided up between Poland and Russia, his family farm ending up in the newly formed Ukrainian Soviet Socialist Republic.

"You seem well-versed in the history of the region, Ruth," said Steve.

"I've always liked history and I've taught it in secondary schools most of my adult life."

"That figures," replied Steve.

Ruth continued by relating how, for a few years, peace seemed to reign and Ostap and his fellow countrymen enjoyed a revival in Ukrainian culture and a renewed sense of identity. It wasn't to last, however, and just before Irina was born, Stalin imposed his infamous five-year plan to industrialise Ukraine. To satisfy the demand for increased food supply, Stalin collectivised the farms, Ostap's family farm included. A large section of the rural population resisted this outrage with the result that hundreds of thousands of so-called kulaks were either murdered or deported to Siberia. The effect this had on agricultural output was devastating. It caused widespread famine and as many as nine million Ukrainians perished in what became known as the Holodomor, the Ukrainian Holocaust. Having survived this terror more was to follow when the Nazis invaded during the Second World War. The Germans and the Russians contrived to outdo each other in the depth of their atrocities. It was then that Ostap could take no more, and with the help of friends in his local authority, managed to smuggle himself, his wife Anna and their child Irina to London.

Steve was not only spellbound by the tale but also by the manner in which she told it. She gave Steve many more personal details, which he would surely incorporate into his obituary of Irina. Ostap was something of a broken man when he arrived in England.

"Let me show you something," she said with excitement in her eyes. Ruth pulled open the drawer of a wooden writing desk and removed a faded copy of a magazine entitled Family for which Irina had given an account of what it was like growing up in a family of immigrants. Steve quickly perused it and found it so interesting that he asked to borrow it. Ruth continued her story. Irina was bright and soon assimilated herself into English society. She had a natural gift for languages and continued to speak Ukrainian with her parents. She eventually met her future husband, Bruce Lockyer while working for the BBC's Monitoring Service in Caversham, near Reading in the 1950s. They had their only child, Ruth, in 1953. Ruth attended a private secondary school near Reading and went on to read history at the University of Birmingham. There followed a postgraduate certificate in education before she embarked on a teaching career.

"I never knew my grandfather, he died before I was born," Ruth explained. "Anna, though, lived on another 10 years and I remember her as a kind, very down to earth eccentric but highly conventional grandmother. I remember that she found all those social changes of the 1960s difficult to come to terms with. It went against everything she was used to in her upbringing."

Ruth explained that she was always close to her mother especially after her father left her for a younger woman in 1971. After Irina returned from a trip abroad in the 1970s, while Ruth was at college, Ruth detected a change in her behaviour.

"She seemed world-wearier and began showing all these obsessive-compulsive traits. We didn't call them that then, of course, but that's what they were and they calmed down after a few months but came back as she started to lose it when she grew old."

Ruth gave several examples of incidents in Irina's life that Steve knew would end up in the obit. She couldn't, to his disappointment, cast any light on what had occurred on that journey, but her father had mentioned at the time that Irina had been seconded to the Foreign Office for a short while. Irina hadn't told him but he'd heard it from a former colleague. This harked back to something Ruth had mentioned when they met in the police station and had set Steve's antennae buzzing.

"I don't know why she never explained what she did but I think she just didn't like talking about her work, you know like soldiers never talked about the war."

Ruth's words merely confirmed a suspicion in Steve's mind that there was much more to this than meets the eye.

Irina retired at the age of 60 and moved to the house in which they were speaking to be nearer to Ruth who was now teaching at a school on the outskirts of London. In their continuing conversation it emerged that Ruth moved in with her mother after Ruth's husband Daniel died of pancreatic cancer five years ago. Yet even to the end, Irina maintained a steely independent core that motivated her to carry out voluntary work at the women's refuge. As Ruth gave more detail, so Steve saw a pattern emerging for his obituary. After more than two hours listening to Ruth's story of her mother, punctuated only by the occasional question, the session ended and Ruth made them both more tea. She then gave Steve a brief conducted tour of the photographs on the living room wall. There were pictures of Irina as a child with her mother Anna and father Ostap in the style of those old Victorian family poses. There were shots of Irina as a young woman, one on horseback taken on a beach holiday and several of her in middle age with Ruth.

"What about your father, Ruth?"

"My father? I don't want to talk about him, thank you very much."

Bruce Lockyer appeared to have been banished from history. Ruth showed Steve several albums of old black and white family photographs that she'd searched for and discovered in attic boxes over the past few days. She'd also looked out her mother's papers but had found nothing that would merit any inclusion in an obituary. Ruth was able to supply Steve with three photographs of her mother in her prime that she thought might best accompany it. She certainly doesn't rate high on the pulchritude scale, thought Steve, but one photograph looked perfect.

Unfortunately, Irina had no surviving relatives but Steve felt that, but for one striking omission, he had virtually everything he needed. He kissed Ruth on both cheeks as he said goodbye and wished her all the best for the funeral. Owing to the circumstances of her death, the authorities had as yet given no date as to when Irina's body would be released. Secretly, Steve was pleased since he hoped that, for once, his obituary might be published before the funeral. It would certainly give those who attended it a much fuller picture of the person to whom they were formally bidding farewell.

Steve believed in striking while the iron is hot and soon after leaving Ruth's door he punched numbers into his phone to call a contact. After a brief conversation he awaited a reply. 15 minutes later the phone rang and his caller supplied the answer for which he had been hoping. With a spring in his step he made his way to the nearby station. As he walked he thought of Irina, alias The Crone, walking this same way only days before. He grabbed a baguette and a desperately required latte from the station café after buying himself a ticket that would take him to Kew Gardens. During a journey that required two changes, he listened back to some of Ruth's words wishing that everyone he interviewed could be so precise, thorough and engrossing. Already Irina's obituary was beginning to take shape in his mind. Arriving at his destination, he began the 15-minute walk through suburban streets and into open parkland with ornamental lakes full of ducks swimming through algae before arriving at the concrete and glass edifice that houses the National Archives. The receptionist summoned his contact and after a handshake and a brief exchange of words, the pair took an escalator up to the first floor where Steve was given a brown paper file on which, in addition to the numeric library code, was marked with the word "Restricted". Steve threw his coat and bag on the chair beside him and took out his laptop placing it beside him on the desk before firing it up. When ready to go, he inhaled a deep breath, said to himself softly "Here goes", and opened the file. It released that musty smell associated with ageing pieces of paper.

It took Steve some time to set his bearings and to decipher which correspondent was from which organisation and to decode the acronyms so beloved by national organisations in the 1970s. As he leafed through each piece of correspondence carefully, a pattern began to emerge that didn't disappoint. The name Irina Lockyer was written in full only twice in the first of some 150 different documents, and named thereafter simply as IL. The file began with detailed and to Steve's eyes dull correspondence between managers of IL's employers at the BBC and with bureaucrats at the Foreign and Commonwealth Office arguing about details of IL's proposed secondment. There was an exchange over details of pay, pension payments, annual leave, travel concessions and the rest. It became more interesting when the details of why IL was so sought after by the members of the FCO became evident and soon the name SIS, the Secret Intelligence Service, began to dominate the correspondence. When Steve had heard Ruth mention the phrase "trades union mission" an alarm had sounded in his head. His instincts had proved right. There followed some very technical data concerning weapons manufacture at a factory in a town called Dniepropetrovsk in Ukraine.

"Ah, the Ukrainian connection," Steve muttered.

He read on. The name Taras Adamchuk first appeared and was to crop up many times. In fact, TA was the focus of this file, more important so far, it would appear, than IL. As Steve read on, he noted the introduction of the CIA to the correspondence. Suddenly IL was becoming more prominent in the discussions. All the while, Steve typed copious notes on his laptop. The next batch of correspondence consisted of detailed conversations between members of the SIS, all of whose names had been blanked out, and members of the Moscow Embassy. IL had indeed been recruited for a specific job. Steve gawped at the revelations unravelling before him.

"So, Mrs Crone, bugger me if you weren't a bit of a spy," said Steve softly to himself. The number of blanked-out names increased as the operation was launched. His attempt at obtaining a clear picture of events was continually frustrated by material relating to airline arrival times, hotel bookings and other routine logistical arrangements. Steve wondered why the registry could not have separated these out. The other main obstacle to Steve's understanding of the course of events unfolding before him was the constant references to telephone calls and Embassy dispatches that were not available to him. To some extent, Steve was piecing together a jigsaw that was incomplete. But gradually as he read on, continually referring back to previous correspondence and with the help of a diagram he sketched on a piece of paper interpreting which person belonged to which organisation, the nature of Irina Lockyer's short operation with MI6 revealed itself. What was inescapable was the contrast between the matter-of-fact tone of the memoranda exchanges and the reality of what was happening on the ground. The only exceptions were the final papers that for the first time contained what to Steve saw as a degree of humanity. Perhaps, thought Steve, the emotion had been confined to the telephone conversations to which he was not privy.

After some three hours of concentrated study, Steve closed the file, packed away his computer, gathered up his belongings and sought out his contact to whom he offered hearty thanks. As he walked back down the stairs out and out into the open air of a warm autumn day in Kew, he decided to delay his return to the office and instead take a stroll around Kew Gardens, his favourite London park where the variety of trees in particular he regarded as the finest he had ever seen particularly now that their leaves were on the turn and displaying their glorious gamut of ripe russets. As he wandered along the pathways flanked by herbaceous borders and towered over by the most exotic of arboreal splendour, he reflected upon this old woman that he and his colleagues had derided as The Crone who had turned out to have been a person with whom he would have loved to have sat down on the train and chatted to about her life. He consoled himself with the notion that the effects of old age would have probably made conversation difficult and that the most interesting episode in her life, at least from an outsider's point of view, was locked inside her anyway. On his return to the office, Steve had great pleasure in informing Harry Fearnley that Irina's obituary would be ready by the end of the week and gave him an indication of what it was likely to contain. He then put in a courtesy call to Frank Butters since he had promised to keep him informed of developments. The call was well received.

15 IRINA AGAIN

"IRINA LOCKYER OBITUARY"

"Irina Lockyer was a shuffling old woman in her 80s who would irritate me and fellow commuters by finding it impossible to sit still for more than a few minutes on the train journeys she took regularly into London. However, in most ways she was just an ordinary old woman struggling to cope with the fast pace of 21st century life with an old-fashionedness derived from a strict background that was reflected in her traditional life view and in her dress sense. It was inconceivable then that such an ordinary and harmless woman should be cast into the media spotlight when unknown gunmen shot her down in cold blood on 5 September outside the women's refuge where she worked as a part-time volunteer. In life, publicity would have been the last thing for which she would have wished. Yet her murder was not the only thing that marked her out from the crowd. A renowned linguist who translated several books into Polish and Ukrainian, Irina Lockyer also harboured a secret of which not even her family was aware. In 1975 she took part in a covert CIA and MI6-backed operation in Ukraine to try to "turn" a Soviet physicist engaged in military research. The mission was to have a lasting effect on her life.

Lockyer's gift for languages stemmed from her upbringing, in the Galicia region of Ukraine. She was born Irina Shevchenko in the town of Stanislav (now called Ivano Frankivsk) on 5 June 1930 and was raised on a smallholding to the west of the town. Stanislav was then part of Poland, the Poles having wrested control of the area from the Austro-Hungarian Empire after World War I and held it following a war with Russia. An only child, the young Irina spoke Ukrainian at home but Polish at school. Being from a nation next door to Hungary and Czechoslovakia, she became familiar with words and phrases from their languages too. Her first years were marked by poverty. Her house had no running water or electricity and food was sometimes scarce. Many of the friends she made at primary school emigrated to a better life in the United States,

South America or Europe. Somehow Irina's family managed to escape the widespread destitution that ensued after Stalin annexed the region and collectivised the farms. Her Uncle Alexei on her mother's side was declared an enemy of the state and became one of thousands to be executed by Stalin's henchmen. Many more died from hunger. Her father, Ostap Shevchenko joined the Organisation of Ukrainian Nationalists and took part in sabotage raids against all the "foreigners" including Poles, Russians, Hungarians and Germans who occupied his land. During World War II, Irina remembers her father speaking about how he witnessed a number of Jews who had been rounded up for deportation to Siberia because they refused to take out Soviet citizenship, being shot by a firing squad by the Russians as the Nazis advanced. When the Nazis unleashed their murderous Operation Barbarossa in Ukraine, Ostap had enough and used a contact to forge the necessary papers to allow him, his wife and child to escape the country for wartime England.

Irina and her family settled in rural Worcestershire away from the ravages of the Blitz and other centres of destruction. Her father found work as a painter and decorator and Irina, by now 12, attended a grammar school in Malvern where she soon assimilated into the language and culture. Yet Irina never knew domestic bliss. Her father, shattered by the tumult and upheaval that had dogged his life, began drinking heavily. In an article Irina wrote in a magazine entitled Family many years later, she described how he would regularly come home drunk and violent. He would administer dreadful beatings to his wife Anna, though he never touched Irina. The only solace her mother and she would find was in knitting. On many an evening as the drunken Ostap collapsed, and after tending to her mother's cuts and bruises, she and Anna would knit away the hours until it was time for Irina to turn in. Sometimes the father would mock them in a drunken rage and unpick a scarf or a jumper and throw the wool about the room. Yet the habit continued and by her mid-teens Irina was so adept that she was winning competitions in her local knitting circle. It was a pastime she enjoyed until the end.

There were periods of sobriety and contrition from her father and Irina benefited from a fine state education with an emphasis on English grammar, which would become invaluable in her future career as a linguist. She left home in 1950 at the age of 19 to work with Ukrainian and Polish refugees in London, helping them with translations. Two years later, she applied successfully to the BBC's Monitoring Service in Caversham near Reading, Berkshire where she translated into English the news output of Ukrainian and Polish radio stations for use by governments and broadcasters. It was here that she met Bruce Lockyer, a translator in the Arabic section, and after Irina became pregnant the two married in 1952. A daughter, Ruth, was born the following year. Ostap attended the wedding but died the same year, never seeing his grandchild.

After taking time off to raise her daughter, Irina returned to the BBC first on a part-time basis, and later full-time once Ruth had finished primary school. In the mid-1970s while the United States and the Soviet Union were still engaged in the Cold War, Irina Lockyer came under the spotlight of MI6. According to papers recently made public at the National Archives, a Soviet scientist named Taras Adamchuk who worked on satellite research in the closed Ukrainian city of Dniepropetrovsk at the heart of the Soviet military industrial complex, was identified by the CIA as being disillusioned with the Soviet authorities over the military application of his work. Adamchuk was a Ukrainian who had a family connection to Irina through her father's side. He was due to take part in a conference in the town of Uzhhorod. With her family ties and her knowledge of the language and the dialects, Irina was identified as the perfect person to convey a message from the Americans and British that they would be willing to help him defect to the West. She did indeed make contact with Adamchuk. However, the CIA's information appeared to be misguided and when Irina, in veiled terms as her handlers had instructed, suggested to Adamchuk that the West might be a much healthier and profitable place in which to work, the scientist was angered and informed the security services. It is not known precisely what occurred next but Irina was subjected to intense interrogation and torture, by being deprived of sleep. Irina never spoke about it except to her handlers in debriefing. What is clear is that Irina did not "crack" and never admitted to be an agent of the British security services, however fleetingly. She was released within days.

According to her daughter, Irina took a long time to recover from her ordeal. Ruth was never made aware of the exact circumstances of it and could never understand why her mother never let on as to what she'd experienced. For many years Irina lost her joie de vivre and developed claustrophobia. She found it difficult to concentrate and the BBC allowed her to revert to part-time working. Her marriage to Bruce Lockyer broke up acrimoniously when her husband admitted to an affair with a younger woman. The couple were divorced in 1979. Irina took up knitting once again seemingly as a way to combat stress. Although she was always of a religious bent, she had never attended Mass on a regular basis. Now, only illness prevented her from missing a service. She was secure financially since, although her daughter never knew it, she was awarded an early pension from the government as a reward for the work she had performed in Ukraine even if the result was not as was hoped. Adamchuk still lives there. Irina also embarked upon several lucrative projects including translating two of Shakespeare's plays, Hamlet and Macbeth into Ukrainian and conversely, translating some of the work of Ukrainian poet Taras Shevchenko (no relation) into English. Though she gradually recovered from her ordeal, her daughter noticed compulsive-obsessive traits returning in old age

Throughout her life, Irina was, in the words of her daughter and colleagues, indefatigable. Never one to accept retirement as a state of mind, she worked for several charities to the very end, never forgetting that her family had often benefited from the kindness and generosity of neighbours when times were tough in Ukraine. Neither did she forget the experience of a violent father, and her work at the women's refuge in which she helped comfort those by teaching them how to knit, and by supplying some of the attendees with warm woollen clothing, stemmed directly from those memories.

Irina Lockyer cut an eccentric figure, finding the vagaries of fashion completely baffling. She was a stickler for grammar and was disenchanted by modern teaching methods. Her championing of the underdog would sometimes conflict with her deeply held conservative views. In her seventies, she invaded the Beaufort Hunt alongside other protestors, and upbraided the Master of the Hounds in no uncertain terms with impeccably choice language and by striking his riding hat with her walking cane. She took pleasure in being arrested and was disappointed not to be charged. It was typical of a woman who had never been cowed by authority, and a woman who had acquired great strength from adversity from which she developed a strong humanitarian core.

Irina Anna Lockyer is survived by her daughter Ruth."

It is common for a death to make the front page of a newspaper with the obituary on the inner pages filling out the life of the deceased. It is rare though for the obituary itself to make headline news. The Herald warned all the other media in advance that Irina, who had clocked up hundreds of column inches in the press and many hours of broadcast time over the progress of the hunt for her murderer or murderers, had been employed by the security services. Steve worked the social networks to herald his scoop. "IRINA WAS A SPY", screamed the headline in The Sun. "IRINA 007", read the Daily Mirror. The Herald said simply, IRINA SPIED FOR BRITAIN and added thousands to its circulation. From being something of a figure of fun after being caught on the CCTV pictures on Belvedere Crescent, Steve was now the toast of the news department. Radio and TV channels across the country clamoured for interviews. Frank Butters was overjoyed, though with typical regard for the command structure, he admonished Steve for keeping him out of the loop for so long even though deep down he recognised that he would have done exactly the same had he been in Steve's position.

There was faint praise too from his own department. Harry Fearnley was not used to having such positive focus on obituaries. Now he too was taking part in media discussions about the art even though he disliked the limelight. There had developed a certain froideur towards Steve from his colleagues over the past months. Ostensibly there was a feeling that the "ordinary person" obituaries belonged in regional newspapers and not in The National Herald and that Steve's approach did not gel with theirs. There was something more "emotional" to his prose, less of the understatement that had previously been a hallmark of the paper's obit style. What they could not admit to was the resentment over the slack that Steve was cut with regard to the time he was given to visit his interviewees to produce his once-weekly obituary. He, unlike they, had less of the tedious fact checking and sub-editing required from the obituaries they commissioned from specialists. In fact, there was less writing, and therefore less creativity to their jobs of which they were at best envious, at worst jealous. To cap it all, Steve's obituaries had achieved a certain celebrity while their efforts appeared less appreciated as a result. Nevertheless, all this was put aside at least temporarily by the fact that Steve's scoop had for a moment put the obituary centre stage and they were going to milk this glory while they could.

Steve left the office that evening after having been interviewed many times and on every occasion with almost the same set of questions. Only once had he felt that he hadn't quite acquitted himself as well as he might. In the last question of the last radio interview a young female presenter asked him if he thought that obituaries represented man's innermost need to reflect on their mortality. His reply was,

"Look, love, I'm just a journalist like you. I see a good story, I find out as much about it as I can, then I write it as best I can. It's like every other story except in my case the subject's dead. Your question might well be true but you need to speak to a philosopher about that."

In retrospect, he knew he'd been brusque and patronising but it had been a long day. With a bit of luck, he thought, not many people had heard it. He tried to concentrate more on the positives and as he walked towards the tube station, he was imbued with a glowing sense that he had achieved something and that colleagues and people who perhaps knew him only by sight were saying to themselves that there goes the man who got today's scoop. Tomorrow it would be business as usual, so enjoy it while you can. He imagined people looking at him with a view to securing his autograph. It was at that point that Steve realised that vanity was going to his head. It was then that his phone rang. It was Ruth.

"Why didn't you tell me about my mother being a spy?"

"Ah, Ruth." Steve swallowed before taking a deep breath. It was a call he had been expecting. "The reason Ruth was that I didn't want to tell you in case you told someone else and the secret leaked out. However, I did try to call you last night to warn you about it but you'd turned off your phone. Same thing happened this morning."

"I turned off my phone to stop reporters from pestering me about my mother's murder case."

"That's what I mean. You could easily have let the cat out of the bag."

"So, you were doing it entirely to protect your scoop."

"Yes, precisely. I am a working journalist, it's what we all hanker for, though in this case it was entirely unexpected."

"Did it never occur to you about what I thought or what my mother would have thought?"

"How do you mean?"

"There must have been a reason why my mother didn't tell me for all those years."

Steve gave a frown of puzzlement as he tried to decipher what Ruth was trying to say.

"And what would that have been?"

"I don't know, I really don't know. I expect it was because my mother didn't want to upset me because it has upset me. The only thing I keep thinking about since I read the obituary was of her being interrogated in a foreign jail and being tortured. I'm very upset and I think she was right. I really didn't want to know that, I really didn't."

Steve paused for thought. "Well I'm sorry it's upset you, Ruth and I can quite understand why you're upset but I think that in the long-term you'll be better off knowing what really happened to your mother and I think you'll agree that now knowing what you know it explains a lot of her behaviour when she came back."

"You may be right but you also may be wrong. Who are you to judge? Didn't it occur to you that I might have been a better judge? She was my mother after all and I have to live with the consequences. You'll just go and do your next bit of work and in a couple of days you'll have forgotten my mother. You should have let me be the judge. You should consider people's feelings instead of just thinking about your blasted scoop."

Steve looked skywards with an air of resignation. "Well I'm sorry you feel that way, Ruth, but believe me I'll be proved right on this one. If your mother had turned out to be an axe murderess, OK I might be wrong but as it turns out she was a hero."

"The point is my mother didn't want this spoken about for whatever reason and you should have respected that wish."

"Well we'll have to differ on that one Ruth. I honestly believe I was right, scoop or no scoop. Can I just thank you again for all your help on this."

"You can thank me, Steve, but I'm not thanking you. Maybe I will as time goes by but not now. Goodbye."

Steve gave a big sigh, put his phone in his pocket and wondered why whenever anything seemed to being going well for him, something always came up to dampen his spirits. However, as he journeyed home, he thought philosophically about Ruth's call and decided that he was an easy target for her anger and that she was probably angry that her mother hadn't ever told her about what had happened to her and angry that she unlike Steve had never bothered to find out. He headed for the station. As he replaced his phone in his pocket, he momentarily lost his balance and collided with a man walking behind him. As he apologised, he couldn't help but notice a hairy wart on the man's nose.

16 THE OGRE

Hilary was late for the train home thanks to a delay on the underground. Clutching her bag close to her side, and checking her watch which, in so doing, gave her enough hope that she might make it in time given a fair wind, she dashed up the metal steps of the escalator, ran as fast as her short legs would carry her along the corridor, sidestepping as she went the droves of commuters streaming towards her. She nearly tripped over a nun, found an infant child entangled with her feet, was hit by three rucksacks as their bearers turned the wrong way to see from where the heavy breathing was coming, and kicked at least two suitcases on wheels. The "sorrys" became almost a continuous flow from her mouth.

"Why," she muttered to herself, "when you're in a hurry does everybody seem to be walking in slow motion?"

At the same time, through her mind raced the thought that those exercise classes she was taking may at last be paying off. She'd never been very sporty. At school she was far more studious than her friends and she was quite devious at finding ways to avoid playing organised games. She was never imbued with the competitive spirit and this was partly why, despite having the wit and mental agility to have succeeded as a barrister, she had settled for the more sedentary life of a solicitor. In the gym, she had only to compete against herself but at this moment she was racing against time. She had one more flight of stairs to endure before she would reach the platform, each step more tiring than the previous. An initial attempt at taking two at a time nearly proved a disaster and was abandoned. She checked her watch again. It was going to be touch and go. If she missed the train she was going to be late at the childminder's for the second time this week. Her husband wouldn't be able to come to her rescue this time since he was staying on for a parents evening at the school where he taught. By now, her lungs were wheezing, her thighs were burning and the sweat was oozing from her brow. She could see the gate in front of her. She could feel the gaze of those she passed. How she wished she were wearing her trainers. Clack clack clack went her platform shoes. With twenty yards to go, she heard the whistle blow. Would they let her through? Surely, they'd let her through. With 10 yards to go, she knew they wouldn't. For, there by the gate, with his ticket machine slung round his neck stood The Ogre. Hilary's heart sank. Just as one could guarantee that the train will never be late when you want it to be, so you can guarantee that if you arrive less than a minute before departure time, The Ogre will be on duty. She smiled as broadly as she could, raising her eyebrows in that expectant kind of way, waving her ticket in front of her and saying, "Please?" Not a chance. The Ogre said not a word, just shook his head and looked away. Hilary knew from past experience that no manner of pleading or haranguing would have the slightest effect. She could have offered him endless riches, unbounded sex; it would have made no difference. What was particularly irksome was that in front of them the driver was still chatting to the guard and was clearly not on the point of departure but when Hilary pointed this out it was to no avail. The rule was that if you arrive less than a minute before the scheduled departure time you were not allowed on and that was that. Rules is rules. Hilary's reaction was typically mild-mannered. She thought to herself that at least the person she would sit next to on the following train wouldn't have to see her sweating profusely. Ben was standing next to the train watching as Hilary was turned away. He clambered on board and took his seat next to Robbie.

"The Ogre's just stopped Hilary getting on. I think it's time we invoked Plan A. Up for it?"

"You bet," Robbie replied.

Plan A for The Ogre, Steve?"

"The Ogre? Oh yes, nice one."

The ticket inspector they called The Ogre had earned his nickname for his lack of a mere scintilla of politeness, for the undue rigour with which he executed his duties and for his permanently stern countenance. The smartness of his uniform was in contrast to the scrofulous nature of his complexion. When people produced their tickets for inspection, he would demand they move their thumb as if they were deliberately concealing the wrong date or station. No matter that he dealt with passengers day after day and appeared not to be suffering from any short-term loss of memory, nobody was trusted. If your ticket was in order, there would be a "That's alright" mumbled in an emotionless monotone with never a "thank you" or God-forbid a "sorry". The irritation and antagonism he succeeded in engendering was for him the pleasure of the job. It was how he measured his day. When he caught someone out, his joy was palpable not by any change in demeanour but with the relish with which he informed his victims of the severity of their financial penalty. Neither flexibility nor common sense were concepts with which he was familiar. He doubtless viewed the expletives that exploded from distraught or frustrated passengers as a vindication of his hard-line, disciplined approach.

Steve had often fantasised, as was his wont, as to what unfortunate childhood influences might have produced such an unappealing personality. Despite being of middle age, Steve imagined The Ogre returning home at the end of each day to look after his wheelchair-bound hypochondriac of a mother who had been systematically emotionally blackmailing him from an early age. She had turned him against his own father particularly after the husband had walked out on his marriage after years of abuse. The message that he must tend first and foremost to her demands or face hell and damnation was reinforced day after day, year after year. She dominated all aspects of his life allowing barely any personality development other than a self-loathing, and rendering any serious relationships with a partner, whether male or female, totally impossible. After the daily evening bible reading that preceded dinner cooked by The Ogre always to his mother's specifications, he would ask her about his work.

“Good day, today, Ma,” he’d reply.

“Caught another cheat this morning. This young cow tried to palm me off with a Saver Plus when I knew that she knew that only a Super Saver was valid before 16.37. I knew she was up to something, you can tell her sort.”

“What a filthy cow!” his mother would reply. Never a “well done, son”, or a “good work my boy” or any other such compliment.

“I hope you gave her a good sorting out, the dirty bitch.”

“You bet, Ma. Gave her the maximum fine. You should’ve seen her face.”

”Wish I had done,” said the mother.

Secretly of course, The Ogre loathed his mother but felt too guilty to realise it. Yet the resentment grew and grew and the only way he could vent his anger was via the passengers whose tickets he inspected. Steve had noticed that while everyone suffered at the hands of this jobsworth, women suffered disproportionately badly. One day, Steve thought, the anger against his mother would boil over and wreak its vicious revenge. It would come when he had had a bad day at the office in which no one had tried to cheat the system, no one had taken the train with the wrongly priced ticket and no one had attempted to board the train at the wrong time. Even worse, there had been no leaves on the line, no wrong kind of snow, no technical malfunctions, no staff shortages, no short-formed trains and thus no overcrowding. It was difficult to imagine but Steve managed it. The Ogre would go home seething with anger and frustration, only to have his mother bicker at him because she needed her pustulous boils soothed straight away even before his complaining could begin, though his only complaint would have been that he had nothing to complain about. When he eventually brought in a bowl of water, he was scolded because it was the bowl taken from the cupboard under the stairs rather than the one from beneath the sink. Never mind the straw that broke the camel’s back, this led to the claw that smote the mammal's crack. The Ogre smashed his fist into his mother's face. Again and again and again he pummelled her until she could castigate him no more. When he realised what he had done, he was consumed with horror and guilt and began to whimper "Ma, Ma, forgive me Ma." Then, at the dead of night with only a full moon to light his way, he wheeled her out of the house, through the deserted backstreets, on to the path that led alongside the railway, up on to the railway bridge, and with a huge effort, tipped her over the wall and on to the track where her human bulk made an horrendous crash. He stood and looked down and, as guilt and grief overwhelmed him, he leapt over to join her, and the two bodies lay side by side waiting for the 05.38 to mangle them completely.

"Ooohhhh," sighed Steve.

"Are you alright, mate? " asked Robbie.

Absolutely. I just imagined The Ogre getting his comeuppance. I feel better now."

"Well, get ready, you're about to feel even better because he's about to get it in reality. You ready?"

"You bet," replied Steve.

As The Ogre approached Ben, he asked to see his ticket. Ben, Robbie and Steve had discovered a cache of used tickets at the station some days previous and had purloined one each having already hatched a plan. Seizing one of these tickets in one hand so that his thumb concealed the date, he showed it to The Ogre without looking him in the face. When The Ogre asked him to move his thumb the act of which revealed the wrong date, Ben could almost smell the excitement it had aroused in him despite there being not a flicker in his countenance. Ben apologised for his supposed offence with the words "Fair Cop. There's no fooling a seasoned pro like you. I should have known better."

"That'll be £42 for a new ticket and another £40 fine for travelling on a train without a ticket," intoned The Ogre.

"No more than I deserve for my terrible indiscretion," replied Ben secretly shocked at the severity of the "fine".

The Ogre, slightly unnerved by the unexpected lack of anger or even disappointment in Ben's response, brought out the "charge sheet" and began writing down Ben's particulars. As he was nearing the end, Ben stopped him.

"Just a minute, I've suddenly realised that my season ticket's in my other pocket. I do apologise, but I've put you to all this trouble for nothing."

The Ogre looked at Ben in a way that might turn some to salt. There was nothing he could do or say. When he came to Robbie and the same thing happened, The Ogre realised what was going on. He went no further, much to Steve's disappointment. Instead, he left the carriage slamming the interconnecting door after him. Much merriment ensued. One elderly gentleman gave Ben the thumbs-up, saying "Well done, son."

Once the excitement had settled down, Robbie compared notes with Steve as to how the police investigation into The Crone's murder was progressing. There was little to tell other than that the police had no other suspects other than the Albanian people trafficking gang. There was some jocular banter about how in fact Albanians had nothing to do with it. The murderer was in reality The Ogre who had shot The Crone because her Senior Rail Card was out of date. In a few minutes he would come crashing into the carriage with a gun and exact revenge on the three of them for the humiliation they had heaped upon him.

"That would make for an exciting end to the day," suggested Robbie.

"I've had enough excitement for one day," replied Ben. "Apart from the fun with our friend The Ogre, just before I left the office I got an email from the widower of a woman whose obit I'd written objecting to the mention of her previous husband."

"Tell me about it," moaned Steve.

"Well since you ask, I will," said Ben with a smile. He continued.

"There's a famous work of art depicting the aftermath of a husband and wife domestic row that was exhibited at the White Cube gallery a few years ago. I say 'famous', it's famous in certain artistic circles; I'd never heard of it. It was called Après moi, le déluge, by Maurice Kyle, ever heard of it?"

The others all shook their heads.

"Anyway, Kyle's installation depicts a kitchen such as you'd find in a kitchen shop on your average High Street but strewn around it are broken ornaments, crockery and remnants of food. It's a sort of a more violent version of Tracy Emin's Unmade Bed, but more symbolic of the chaotic human condition. Anyway, the woman who inspired the piece with whom he'd had a row, died the other day and I wrote a short obit for the website that centred on her connection with this artwork. The obit had only been posted for about half an hour when her widower, her second husband, emails me questioning why when she was a beautiful woman, wife, lover, mother and all that, do we have to mention this drunken bastard Kyle who had abused her and who she'd left after only a few months anyway? It was a classic case of the media having very different priorities to a grieving husband. Frankly, if this woman hadn't been the one who had helped inspire this work of art, she would never have got an obit. And he couldn't understand why it was labelled a work of art anyway but that's another story."

"So did you reply to him?" asked Robbie.

"No, and I don't think he was expecting me to. He just wanted to make a point."

Steve continued the theme.

"I've had a couple of cases where the families have taken exception to the mention of a previous marriage that ended badly. You know the kind of thing; man marries woman, after six months she has an affair with someone else, they get divorced but she has a good lawyer who manages to sting husband for huge amounts of maintenance that she doesn't deserve, that kind of thing."

"You can understand them though for wanting to blank her out, can't you Steve?" said Robbie.

Steve shifted slightly in his seat, straightened his back and embarked upon what was to sound like a short lecture.

"But like it or not, Robbie, you can't just ignore history. It might be painful for the present, but for the future, and obituaries are in a way like written memorials, it would be dishonest to pretend the marriage never happened. You see it everywhere you go, not just in obituaries but also in so many aspects of life, this desire to wish history away. For example, when I lived in East Berlin in the 1980s, there was a story, a piece of living history actually, that I always relate to families who want to airbrush someone or other out of an obituary."

Robbie and Ben both were both listening intently. Neither knew Steve had lived in East Germany.

"In 1945 Berlin was in ruins after the relentless Allied bombing and the Russian invasion. Most of the historic buildings ended up in East Berlin that the Russians occupied. When the war was over and East Berlin became part of the GDR, the German Democratic Republic, which as we know was part of the Soviet bloc, they carefully restored many of the damaged buildings to their former state. There are whole quarters of the town that were painstakingly reconstructed. But right in the heart of the city was the badly damaged Berliner Schloss, a Palace that had been there for 500 years and was a jewel in the architectural heritage of the city. It was Berlin's equivalent to say St Paul's in London or St Peter's Basilica in Rome. But because the Schloss had been the seat of Prussian emperors, the Russians decided on ideological grounds to pull it down even though the basic structure was still sound. As a result, not only did the city lose one of the most beautiful buildings in Europe, but also 500 years of history went down the toilet."

"Ideological retribution to them, cultural vandalism for the rest I suppose," Ben interjected.

"Absolutely right. In its place, the Russians built a modernist structure to house the East German parliament. But they also opened it out to the people so that they included a bowling alley, a cinema and a dance floor. In fact, I used to go there for a Saturday night out. They called it the Volk's Schloss or something like that, a palace for the people. But then after the wall came down in 1989, the German government decided that once again, we're not having any of that Communist crap, so they pulled down the building leaving just an empty space. Their excuse was that it was full of asbestos, which it was, but they could have stripped it out and refurbished it but no, they didn't want a major symbol of Communism remaining in the heart of their city. Getting their own back, if you like. Now they're going spend billions of Euros rebuilding the Berliner Schloss again exactly as it was.

"Yes, they rebuilt that wonderful church in Dresden a few years back," said Robbie.

"And the Royal Palace in Warsaw and the Salvation Cathedral in Moscow," added Steve.

"But on the other hand, they have kept bits of the Berlin Wall as a reminder," said Ben.

"Yes, in spite of every awful thing it represented. But it happened, nevertheless and like it or not, you can't change that."

Steve continued. "So it's not just governments that try to rewrite history, families do it too. Like with stepchildren. If a second husband say inherits a child when that child is a baby and he brings it up as his own, he gets used to it being his child and calls it his son or his daughter. When I first started writing obits I was sorting out the survivors of someone I was writing about and I'm given the names of his two daughters. I didn't think anything of it except to get the spelling right because that's another touchy thing when you spell someone's name wrong."

"I know that from bitter experience," said Ben.

"Anyway, after the obit's been published I get a call from an angry father demanding to know why I'd put Carol, or whatever her name was, down as a daughter and not a stepdaughter. He then tells me that she was his child and that he paid maintenance for her up to the age of 18 and went to see her in school plays and so on and wasn't just the absent father. Of course, that meant that not only had the family not been honest about the stepdaughter but also that I'd managed to miss another marriage somewhere along the line. So I learnt two things from that episode namely ask more questions of more people to narrow down your chances of missing something like that, and don't always trust what the family tells you because apart from wanting to deliberately block someone out, they can simply get details wrong."

Ben began nodding his head. He knew only too well the pitfalls of taking every piece of family information on trust. He took up the thread.

"Yes, and apart from getting things wrong, they seem strangely ignorant of some of the things about their loved ones. For example, I was doing an obit for the website last year and whoever it was I was writing about, I can't remember who now, had won some award, a quite prestigious one I remember, but I didn't have the date. I had the son's number, so I thought I'd save time looking it up by asking him. He not only didn't know the date, he didn't even know his father had won it. Said something like he was always winning awards so we didn't really take enough notice."

"Goodness, I never realised what a minefield you two operate in sometimes," said Robbie, adding "I wish we could airbrush The Ogre out of history."

As if on cue, the man in question walked back through the train having subjected his passengers to his forensic examination of their travel worthiness. As he passed the three commuter friends he subjected them to an icy stare. As he left their carriage, Robbie and Ben burst out laughing not caring in the slightest whether or not he heard them. Steve would have laughed too were it not for the fact that behind The Ogre walked a younger man, looking at the floor as he moved as if trying not to be recognised. It would have been easier were it not for the fact that he sported a hairy wart on his nose. Could it be the same person who he had seen the other day after leaving work? Just how many people have hairy facial warts? Was this man following him? Steve decided that The Crone business was making him paranoid. As the train reached their destination, Ben asked, "Anybody fancy giving me a lift?"

"Oh God, chain gone again?" said Steve.

"You guessed it," was Ben's reply.

"Ever thought of buying a new chain?" Robbie suggested tentatively.

"I think about it all the time but the bike shop opens after I leave for work and closes before I get home, so the only chance I get is at the weekend. And I always seem to forget at weekends."

"Aren't there any in London?" asked Steve.

"Not where I work, it's nothing but shopping malls with big chain stores."

"Chain stores? That's what you need isn't it?"

"Fuck off."

17 GORDON

"Don't step in that puddle, William."

Steve's words only led to William suspending his yellow Wellington boot over the surface of the water.

"It might not be a puddle, William, it might be a big hole that goes right down to the sewers and you'll fall down and have to live with all the rats and the crocodiles."

At that, William stamped his foot hard into the puddle splashing the muddy contents within a millimetre of his father and sister. Healthy scepticism worthy of a budding journalist, thought Steve. Either that or a father with no natural authority. At least his decision to make his kids wear their boots on the journey had been vindicated.

"Are there really rats and crocodiles in the sewers?" asked Naomi.

"There are definitely rats, big fat smelly ones. But the crocodiles are above ground and there's one coming towards you now," at which Steve grabbed his daughter at the waist and twirled her round. Naomi screamed with laughter and demanded a repeat performance followed, predictably, by William's demands for the same. After giving them three twirls each, the three continued tramping their way to school.

"What are the sewers for?" asked Naomi a few minutes later.

"Well every time you let out the bathwater or flush the toilet, it all goes down to the sewer under the ground and our sewer joins up with a bigger sewer and then a bigger one and then it all gets washed out to sea."

"Errrrgggghhh," she replied. "Does that mean when we go swimming, we're swimming in poo?"

"Well the poo's usually been mixed with lots and lots of water so it isn't really so pooey any more."

"Angela Brown told me that when she went swimming in Spain she saw some poo floating in the sea."

Steve was beginning to regret ever mentioning sewers.

"Well, sometimes that happens, yes."

"Does it make the fish ill if they eat poo?" asked William.

"I don't think fish eat poo, William".

"But if they do, when we go to the fish and chip shop, we might be eating someone's poo."

"Yes but the poo will have been cooked then," was the reply that Steve regretted making as soon as he'd uttered it.

"Errrrgggghhhh," said Naomi again.

"I'm never eating fish and chips again."

"And I'm never swimming in the sea again," said William.

"Well that buggers our next sea-side holiday," thought Steve.

He was still thinking about holidays an hour or so later as he walked towards his caffeine fix.

"A double espresso for me, Gloria," Steve shouted as he passed through the door of Espresso Bongo. There was only one other customer in the café and the absence of the almost permanent sibilance of the steamer was something of a relief.

"And no smart-alick remarks from you either, Doreen."

"Ooooh, touchy are we this morning? Been caught following old women again, have yer?" replied Doreen with a smile.

Steve shrugged his shoulders. “So you heard about that did you?”

"Not often we get people in here whose pictures are on the front page of the papers."

“Well I wasn’t following her, as you well know. Anyway, I blame you.”

"How come?"

“I reckon it was something Gloria put in the coffee. There was I minding my own business when I see this old woman I recognise from my train and something, I don’t know what, made me curious about where she worked. If I hadn’t had my double caffeine boost I wouldn’t have got myself into trouble.”

Both girls laughed and Doreen turned to her colleague. “Blimey. Gloria, make him a cuppa tea or Gord knows what he’ll get up to this time,” she said, still laughing.

“No I’ll stick with the espresso if you please, Gloria. I could do with some excitement today.”

“I’ll give him a single shot and he might follow a woman more of his age,” said Gloria with a cackle.

She banged out the grindings from the coffee holder, filled it with a fresh helping, attached it to the machine before pressing a button that released the water to percolate through. “That poor woman, she was the one who turned out to be a spy, wasn’t she?” asked Doreen.

“That’s right, though she wasn’t exactly Mata Hari,” replied Steve.

“Mata who?” said Doreen bemused.

“Mata Hari. Now there was a woman! She was a high-class prostitute during the First World War who spied for France and Germany and who got her information by sleeping with their top military brass.”

“Sounds like your Auntie Doris, Glor.” The two girls shrieked with laughter. Even Steve couldn't help but join in as Gloria handed his coffee to him.

"Well I hope it wasn't like your auntie because when she came to Britain we executed her," he said as he handed over the money.

"Anyway, " continued Doreen, "Have they caught that poor old girl's killers yet?"

"Not yet. They reckon it's some Albanian criminal gang who'd smuggled those two African girls for the sex trade."

"And then there's that Carla Wilson too. What a world, eh?" sighed Doreen before serving another customer who had entered the shop.

Steve sat down and as he took his first sip began thinking about how unhappy Maria had been at his decision to stay away tonight. He was travelling to Kent that evening to speak to friends of a well-known businessman who had died a couple of weeks ago. They were gathering in one of his favourite pubs in the evening to honour him. Steve had told his wife that he would doubtless have to share a few drinks with them and that the session could well go on until late and that he would be better off staying locally. The first part of his excuse was true. To assuage his guilt he'd taken the kids to school again and said he might be able to rearrange his working schedule to enable him to do so on a regular if not permanent basis. He wasn't really sure, though, that he'd be able to fulfil his suggestion. His colleagues were becoming increasingly resentful of his unofficial flexi-time so he had to walk something of a tightrope in trying to keep his relations with them more harmonious. He checked his emails and the latest tweets on his phone, took a final sip of his espresso, got up and waved goodbye to the coffee girls.

"Mind how you go," shouted Doreen.

"Mind where you go and all," called Gloria laughing.

The light was beginning to fade on this relatively warm afternoon. Steve decided to walk the few miles to Victoria Station where he would catch the train to Rochester. He enjoyed strolling around London, discovering little parks and monuments impossible to notice on public transport. Those blue plaques on the walls of houses denoting where everyone from South American revolutionaries to famous English authors once resided intrigued him. He reached The Embankment and paused for a few minutes to watch the ferries laden with commuters and day-trippers chugging their way up the Thames on their way towards Greenwich. The autumn sun was reflecting off the honey-coloured Palace of Westminster to his right and on the left the pods of the London Eye opposite sparkled in the sunlight. As he walked the straight road with Big Ben directly in front of him, with a warm southwesterly breeze caressing his face, he was thinking what a glorious city London can be in the soft autumnal glow. A family of Chinese tourists had assembled against the concrete parapet on the river's side of the road, and the father asked Steve if he wouldn't mind taking their picture. With a smile he duly obliged, squeezing the three children and parents into the frame against the backdrop of the river. Then everything changed. As he swung his gaze to view the river from the other direction he caught side of the same person whom he had seen twice before, the one with the hairy wart. The man, recognising that he had been spotted, sidled off quickly and vanished from view amid the rush of people. Steve felt a ripple of fear convulse through his being like the wake from the Thames barge he had just watched sail past him. Two sightings may have been a coincidence but three could only signify that he was being followed. He spotted a nearby bench and sat down to gather his thoughts. His worst fear, until now buried albeit near the surface, was that those Albanians were after him, trying to eliminate him, a potential witness to their presence staking out the house in Belvedere Crescent. He decided to phone the police, specifically DCI Medlock, the officer who had interviewed him initially. He knew he had her card somewhere in his wallet. He found it and put in the call. She wasn't available but her deputy, DI Beavon came on the line. In an anguished tone of voice Steve described the scenario and expressed his fears about the Albanian threat. DI Beavon appeared sympathetic but told him that unless a crime was being committed there was little they could do at the moment. Steve was not happy.

"Does that mean they have to shoot me first before you'll act? Is that my understanding? Can we arrange a one-word code perhaps so that in my dying breath I can phone you and you'll understand what has happened in case I can't finish the sentence?" DI Beavon tried interjecting but Steve was by now manic. He continued, "If they shoot me in the mouth, maybe there's a certain syllable we can agree on, shall we say 'ooof' or something like that?"

The detective eventually did his best to calm Steve down. He asked a few questions regarding the man's appearance. He said he'd check his database for anyone sporting a hairy nasal wart. He also advised him that if he saw him again to call him or DCI Medlock immediately. He also made suggestions that if he did appear again that Steve should try and catch sight of a registration number if he was driving or snap him with his camera phone.

"Shall I get him to say 'cheese' as well?". The detective then tried to ease Steve's mind by saying that they had already made one arrest and that they were confident that from the information they had received from the Nigerian girls, from the forensic evidence at the scene including the bullet cases, and a car with a registration that included the letters SG which they had connected to one of the suspects, that they had known for some time who they were looking for and it was only a matter of time before they would arrest them all. It didn't help. Steve bade a grudging goodbye and the idea that he was being hunted down dominated his mind as he made his way to Victoria. Every few yards he looked around trying to spot his pursuer. Twice he deliberately broke into a trot to see if anyone behind him was spurred to do the same. Eventually, he was satisfied that he'd managed to shake off whoever it was. Nevertheless, before boarding the train at the station he again surveyed the platform looking for the hairy wart. Steve was almost oblivious of the wretched condition of this commuter train, though as he reached his destination he made a mental note not to criticise his own rail company quite so much.

On his arrival in Rochester he took a taxi to the Bird in Hand pub in the centre of the town. It was one of those ugly dark brown brick urban affairs with maroon tiles that were more suited, he thought, to a public toilet. From its walls hung an absurd number of flowering baskets that were reaching the end of their lifespan with large clusters of dead leaves hanging from the stems beneath. Inside wasn't much better. The faded yellow wallpaper looked as if it hadn't been replaced in decades, grimy with ingrained smoke and tar from all those years before the smoking ban. As Steve entered the saloon bar he saw a group of a dozen or so, mostly middle-aged and older that he guessed were the friends of Gordon Gunter, or GG, as he was universally known, the man in question. They were all white and had commandeered a whole section of the saloon bar and were laughing and joking vociferously as Steve arrived through the door. GG had died a relatively wealthy man, a seemingly perfect example of a poor Cockney boy done good. He'd grown up in the east end of London from humble origins but had been blessed with enough business sense to have built up a highly successful and exclusive limousine service for the rich and famous. That's about all Steve knew of him other than that he'd died of a heart attack at the age of 75. He'd been sent a brief and rather inarticulate life summary from one of Gunter's friends who introduced himself to Steve when he entered the pub.

"How did you know who I was?" joked Steve as he shook hands with Harold Grayson.

"We can smell the media round here," he replied to a few chortles.

Steve thanked everyone for inviting him and said how much he was looking forward to hearing about their friend's life. It transpired that The Bird in Hand was once GG's favourite watering hole before he moved onward and upward, but it was here that many of his business deals had been clinched. Steve then ordered a round of drinks that consisted almost exclusively of beer for the men and a couple of Bacardi and cokes for the two ladies present. Steve ordered a pint of best for himself. After his anxieties over pursuing Albanians he was in need of several and he knew that tonight he was going to get them. It turned out that GG was the only surviving member of his nuclear family, save for a brother and that a cousin was the only family member present. He hoped that the cousin would know such details as where and when he was born, his first job and the rest. There were a couple of men who'd known him since schooldays. Most of the others were former employees including some chauffeurs and a secretary.

Once he'd carried the drinks over Steve asked the question that he tended to begin with at all such gatherings, "What are your abiding memories of GG?"

Harold began. "Well, he was the salt of the earth was GG."

There was much nodding in agreement while inside Steve groaned. He'd managed to reach what he called Cliché Corner within record time. He began to recite all the usual ones in his mind as Harold wittered on.

"He was always there for you, he'd do anything for anybody, he only saw the best in people, was generous to a fault, larger than life, always a gentleman, never suffered fools, strict but fair, broke the mould, never complained, left the world a better place, one of a kind, heart of gold, always gave 110%, never had a bad word to say about anyone, a child at heart, ahead of his time, iconic, a legend, a role model, not a churchgoer but very spiritual, a knight in shining armour, he lived each day as if it was his last." Well he got the last one right eventually, thought Steve. Yet, as often happened, once the conversation progressed and stories were told and more alcohol was consumed, the more three-dimensional GG became. Steve took notes rather than use a recorder since it was easier in that way to determine who was saying what. Early on he learnt one interesting aspect of GG.

"Did he have a wife or wives?"

There was a general chuckle.

"GG was not one for the ladies, but it wasn't something that we were encouraged to talk about, " said Harold with mock tact. "But now he's dead...." There was much laughter as Harold's statement opened the floodgates to a lot of crude and homophobic descriptions of GG's sexual preferences not all of which were legal, and a man called Alan summed him up as a "right roaring Queen". He had a partner with whom he lived latterly and who had died two years ago. Steve gathered anecdotes and opinions about various aspects of GG's character from different eras of his life. In order to gain some colour, Steve had a few stock questions at the end. These included such matters as to what kind of build he was, any peculiar mannerisms, any stock phrases he might have used, whether or not he smoked, his outside interests, his tone of voice, whether he was an introvert or extrovert. There was a quite buzz about the place as one story would provoke another and friendly disagreements broke out over the intricacies of each one. After a couple of hours and several pints later, more and more details emerged about a dark side to Gordon's character, how he and his brother would intimidate people. Gradually the positive clutch of clichés that opened the conversation seemed to dissipate ever more into the background. However, there was one more to end with before the assembly had to move on to a party being thrown, again in GG's honour. Steve was invited but felt he had more than enough to go on and politely declined the offer. As he got up, a man called Alan, a somewhat rough looking character, the type you wouldn't want to meet in the proverbial dark alley at night, mused, "Old GG, in spite of everything, he'd give you the shirt off his back." There was a general murmur of agreement. Then Steve, who had forgotten to include that one in his mental list, and emboldened by an excess of ale, looked at Alan and said, "That shirt you're wearing, is that the one he gave you off his back?" Steve was smiling but Alan's face suddenly turned sour. He fixed Steve with an icy stare. The room went quiet. A moustachioed man rose to his feet instinctively at the sign of trouble. After a few seconds pause Alan said,

"Are you takin' the piss, mate?"

Steve was taken aback. "No, I was just..."

"Are you patronising me?" continued Alan. Everyone was looking at Alan who was standing up and drawing his face ever closer to Steve's head.

"Easy Alan," said Harold with a worried expression. Alan took no notice.

"You trying to be funny?"

The words were given more threat by the silence that now enveloped this part of the room. Steve felt his lower bowel loosen and sweat poured into his palms and on to his face, his by now very pale face.

"Honestly, Alan, I wasn't trying to be funny..."

Before he could finish his sentence, Alan put his face right next to Steve's in the most threatening of manners and then planted a big wet kiss directly on to his mouth.

"Well you was quite funny as a matter of fact," said Alan and burst into laughter. The rest of the group followed suit as much out of relief as of being amused.

"Had you there didn't I?" Alan screamed at Steve with a huge smile on his face.

"Had you all, didn't I?" he added turning to the others.

Steve gulped his beer as the laughter continued and Alan slapped him hard on his back nearly causing him to projectile vomit over the saloon bar. He'd never been so pleased to be kissed by a man. As the individuals got up to leave, Steve shook hands with everyone. He then ordered a taxi and went hurriedly to the toilet. After a few minutes during which he looked at himself in the mirror and vowed never again to make a remark such as the one he'd just made about the shirt, he returned to the bar, which was now almost empty, and prepared to settle his tab. As he was taking his wallet from his jacket pocket, he was then taken aback by the words of the barman.

"I've been listening to what all them blokes have been saying about GG. I've been working in this bar for years and I've known him since he first started coming here. I'm not saying I didn't like him, he was fun and all that but I can tell you he could be a hard bastard."

"Oh really, that's becoming the consensus view it seems to me."

"Well you don't get where he got in the east-end without shall we say, using a bit of muscle. Don't take my word for it, read the court records."

"What court records?" said Steve, eyes widening.

"In 1962 he was in court for intimidation or summat, can't remember exactly what the charge was. Can't remember what the verdict was come to that but he wasn't quite the Little Lord Fauntleroy that some of those blokes would have you believe."

"I was beginning to get that impression," Steve sighed. "Are you certain of the year, 1962?"

"Yes I'm absolutely certain. It was the same year he got done for nobbing."

"Nobbing?"

"Yes, up on the Heath."

"Ah, got you," said Steve even more wide-eyed. "What was his sentence?"

The barman chuckled. "He got the minimum fine 'cos he recognised the judge who used to nob in the same places he did." Steve laughed, shaking his head again.

"I know it was 1962," continued the barman, "cos one of the blokes who took him to court was my future brother-in-law and I got married that year and he wasn't able to make the wedding because he was in court, like."

Steve took out his notebook from his pocket. "What was the date of your wedding, um, sorry I don't know your name."

"Don't worry about my name. I got married on the 14th August 1962."

"And where did these events take place?"

"Nobbing was on Hampstead Heath and the other thing was in Hackney I think."

Steve jotted down the appropriate notes. "Well that's very good of you to let me know, whatever your name is. I much appreciate it."

"That's alright. I could never trust him you know, he had a side to him that he didn't often show."

"A side?"

"Yes, like he said, he could be a hard bastard if he wanted to be. And then there was the young boys."

"What?"

At that, the barman tapped his nose and declined to say any more despite Steve's persistent attempts to persuade him to do so. Steve settled his bill, and noticed through the window his cab pulling up. He grabbed his bag and coat and wandered out of the pub a much happier man than he had been five minutes earlier. The barman had delivered him something more to get his teeth into though it would take a trip to the local library or newspaper office to check the archive. He looked around for any hairy warts, saw none, closed the taxi door and ordered the driver to take him back to the station for the trip back to London.

18 GG

"So this fellow Gunter was a homosexual was he?"

Harry Fearnley, Steve's boss, was posing a rhetorical question as he stood bracing himself like a sergeant major next to Steve who was seated at his desk.

"Is that relevant?" he continued.

"How do you mean?" asked Steve.

"Just because he was caught with his trousers down with another man doesn't mean it necessarily has to go in his obituary. If it had no impact upon his career, what's it got to do with the price of fish?"

Steve thought for a moment.

"You're right up to a point. Just because someone's gay doesn't mean you have to make anything of it unless they campaigned for gay rights or whatever."

Harry turned and headed for the bookcase in the middle of the office.

"I think being gay will feature in Gordon Gunter's though since it fits perfectly into the narrative as you will see when I've written it," Steve added.

Harry surveyed the second shelf of the bookcase for a moment before pulling out a slim volume on the history of the obituary and began leafing through its pages.

"You know, one of the obituaries that changed the course of the modern art form was written in 1986 about Sir Robert Helpmann, the famous Australian ballet dancer and choreographer. The Times described him thus." Harry began reading.

“His appearance was strange, haunting and rather frightening. There were, moreover, streaks in his character that made his impact on a company dangerous as well as stimulating. A homosexual of the proselytising kind, he could turn young men on the borderline his way.”

Steve looked quizzical. Harry stopped reading and looked at Steve.

“Now whether you can turn someone your way in terms of sexuality is a separate point but I ask you, was it really necessary to mention all that?”

“This was the guy who played the Child Catcher in Chitty Chitty Bang Bang and frightened to death all those kids of a certain age. Whoever wrote that was probably one of them,” said Steve.

“So you wouldn’t have included it?”

”Yes I would, assuming it was true. Since he was clearly a very dominant personality, it demonstrates an aspect of his personality rather well. You’ve got to keep it in perspective though and put it against all his achievements. You don’t get knighted for nothing, I suppose....unless you’re a civil servant with a fat index-linked pension or a millionaire rock star.”

Harry replaced the book on the shelf

“The point about the Helpmann obit, Steve, is that though it infuriated people at the time, it ended that unspoken rule that you don’t speak ill of the dead in obituaries. I’m all for that but at the same time I think some papers have gone too far because they know the dead can’t sue. I’m not too fond of all this obitchery myself. I just wonder whether one would have said the same sort of thing said about Helpmann about a straight man.”

”Of course we would. Our obituaries are full of heterosexual shaggers.

Look at that Conservative Member of Parliament Alan Clark who managed to shag three women in one family, the two daughters and the mother. It says a lot about the guy. Christ, he was even obsessed with Margaret Thatcher's ankles for God's sake."

"The point I'm making," continued Harry, "is that if someone is doing what he's doing privately without affecting his career, then we should respect that. Someone like Alan Clark revelled in it and lots of his conquests made the TV news."

"Well I don't think it's going to be a problem with our Mr Gunter," said Steve getting to his feet. "Though I take your point, Harry."

Despite being an entirely different character to him, Steve had a healthy respect for his boss. He admired the fact that he was so "hands off" and would seldom question his judgements about what he would and would not include in an obituary even if he were not in full agreement. His little turn with the Helpmann example was typical of his gentle editorial guidance.

"It's time I was off, Harry. I've got to go to Ilford to check out his court appearance in the Hackney Messenger archive and then up to Hampstead to the Ham and High.

"Got a record, this Gunter has he?"

"Apparently so, but I've got to check it out."

"Well good luck and watch your back."

This last remark referred to the Hairy Wart that Steve had spoken to Harry about. This tufty epidermal blemish had come to embody the man as a whole. As soon as he left the Herald's glass-fronted reception, he hailed a cab. After giving the driver the directions, Steve installed himself in the back. The driver had left the sliding door that separated him from his passenger slightly ajar.

"You're the bloke what got mixed up in that murder, ain't yer?" he inquired of Steve in his thick Cockney accent.

“That’s right,” Steve responded with a sigh.

“They reckon it’s them Albanians, right?”

“That’s what they reckon, yes.”

”You know what I think of them Albanians?”

“No, pray tell,” answered Steve preparing himself for the inevitable racist onslaught.

“I fink that their inclination towards organised crime is ‘cos they was subjected to years of oppression and corruption under their dictator Enver Hoxha.”

Steve’s mouth opened slightly and he started to listen properly.

“It stands to reason, don’t it,” continued the taxi driver. “If you’re given no political opportunity to channel your resentment by a one-party corrupt system and you’re kept in the dark ages an’ all and you know that countries next door are miles better off than what you are, well it’s the politics of envy innit. No wonder that some of the bad ‘uns are gonna resort to crime. And once you do that and you find you’re making loads of dosh out of it, you’ve got the habit, ain’t yer. I’m not justifying it, mind, but I can see how it can happen.”

Steve was pleasantly taken aback. “Well indeed,” he said. “That’s a refreshing viewpoint well made.” The taxi driver hadn’t finished. “I mean it all starts wiv the breakdown of aufority at local level, don’t it. You get corrupt party officials who no one likes, the police are all bent and then you get local outlaws who react against it, the local people support him and sooner or later you’ve got a local warlord. That’s what you’ve got in Afghanistan, ain’t yer, and in Somalia and all them types of places where central government has done a bunk.”

”Yes, the good old power vacuum,” said Steve.

“I mean even ‘ere in London you had the Krays and the Richardsons who used to look after their communities in a way the local bill never done. They got power that way and once you’ve got power, it corrupts, right?

“Right, “ answered Steve and continued, “Don’t suppose you’ve ever heard of a bloke called Gordon Gunter?”

“No, who’s he?”

”No matter, just someone whose obituary I’m researching.”

It was worth a try, thought Steve who was then given more of the taxi driver’s treatise on world problems, so much so that by the time he reached Ilford he was ready to take a masters degree in international relations.

He tipped the taxi driver well and walked into the offices of the Hackney Messenger where he had made an appointment with the archivist. She led the way into a musty windowless basement area where stood a row of microfiche readers. After a basic lesson in how to operate them, she left Steve alone to find what he was looking for. Microfiche readers, in Steve’s experience, always seemed to have a mind of their own and would speed through rows of newspaper columns with a mere twitch of the hand. This one proved no exception and he felt like he was trying to lasso a fish. Nevertheless, once he’d brought it under control, it wasn’t long before he discovered the account of the court case involving Gordon Gunter. Steve’s spirits rose as he read it through carefully, deciding to take notes rather than work out how he could print it. It was of particular benefit since in his conclusion, the reporter made mention of GG’s previous conviction on Hampstead Heath, thus saving Steve another journey. After half an hour or so, his work was complete and with an air of satisfaction, he collected together his belongings and made a courtesy call to the archivist. However, when he arrived at her desk, the paper’s editor was there to greet him. He introduced himself as Roy Choudhury and said how delighted he was to meet the “esteemed” obituaries writer of the National Herald. Steve was appropriately flattered but his journalistic instincts were raised by the next question.

"And to what do we owe the pleasure of your visit to us today?"

"Just a private matter, nothing of any importance," replied Steve.

There was no way a local rag was going to spike his story. Mr Choudhury, with an equally sceptical brain, didn't believe Steve's line.

"Come now, Mr Graham, you have no need to worry, we're hardly competitors."

"No, really, I was just checking out some facts of a woman who was in court here in the 1960s, a friend of my mother's. In fact, there was nothing here that I didn't already know. However, it was very nice of you to make me so welcome. Cheers."

With that, Steve made his way out briskly, looked for a black cab, and when he saw one to hail, he hoped his return journey was not going to be a lecture on the crisis of capitalism or the reasons for the fall of the Babylonian empire. The driver who picked him up chose a different route to the previous cabbie.

"Do you normally drive this way? Steve asked him.

"Nah mate, I normally sit on the roof but since it's raining...."

Three days later, the following obituary appeared in the Herald.

GORDON GUNTER, THE "LIMOUSINE LIZARD"

Gordon Gunter, known by friends and acquaintances simply as GG, but by the business world as "The Limousine Lizard" has died of heart failure at the age of 75. During the "swinging sixties", Gunter pioneered the use of limousines for special occasions in London. His pink stretched Lincoln Continental, often with him at the wheel, became a familiar sight at

West End premieres and at large sporting occasions. His limousines were derided as garish, brash and vulgar by many at the time but adored by celebrities such as Judy Garland, Liberace, Tony Curtis and Shirley Bassey. When the photographer Henri Luc Besson famously snapped Liz Taylor flashing a V-sign at a posse of paparazzi, she was leaning out of one of Gunter's limousines. Equally famous was the decision by the owners of the Ascot racecourse to ban Gunter's pink limo from entering the course in 1964 while The Queen was present, considering it to be in bad taste. The decision provoked many columns of newsprint on taste determinants and Britain's class system. Today, the plethora of limousine companies offering over-stretched and colourful limousines for stag nights, school proms, weddings, funerals, parties, birthdays, corporate and sporting events owe a debt of gratitude to Gordon Gunter for his groundwork in making this American idea acceptable in Britain.

Gordon Reginald Gunter was born in Dalston, in the east end of London, in April 1935. When he was five, he became an evacuee with his younger brother Fred. The pair spent time on a Somerset farm but after falling off a horse twice, breaking his arm each time, and injuring his foot after stepping on a gin trap, his parents decided that it would be less dangerous to bring him back to Blitz-torn London. Once the war had ended, his mother, Queenie Gunter, began running a fruit and veg stall in the local market and on weekends and during the holidays Gordon would help her on the barrow. He loved the buzz of the local community, could gossip for hours with the women market workers and he soon learnt the kind of sales patter that would serve him well in later years. He would as often as not wear a bow tie, an extraordinary item of apparel for a market trader but one that reflected his outlandish nature. He took great pride in his dapper appearance and even as an adolescent his trademark red silk handkerchief was seldom absent from his top pocket. He wore lashings of his favoured Old Spice after-shave. As one friend told me, "You could smell him coming from 10 miles away." GG was a bear of a man, more than six foot three, with a gentle voice that somehow didn't quite match. It was said that his mother, Queenie G as she was known, was at times frustrated by Gordon's tendency to shoot off to the local cinema to indulge his love of the movies, in particular the Hollywood musicals. He would occasionally annoy other cinemagoers by munching loudly on his Cox's pippins purloined from his mother's stall.

However, when Gunter left St Aloysius Secondary Modern School in 1950, he went straight to work in his father's scrapyard. Ronald Gunter had established a certain local reputation. A well-known expression in the East-End at the time if you had an old crock of a car was "send it to Gunter's" or "that ain't fit for Gunter's". Here the young Gordon learnt all there was to know about cannibalising motors to rebuild scrapped cars. It was while he was messing about "stretching" an old crock with a welder and a few pieces of scrap metal that he first formed the idea of venturing into the limousine business. He imported his first Lincoln Continental in 1961, with money borrowed from his father, having seen them in the movies. They appealed to his sense of the extravagant. He began hiring it out and it proved successful enough that within a year he had increased his fleet to three. Gunter was admired for his bonhomie and his gregariousness but there was a ruthless side to his personality when it came to business. In 1962, he was accused of destroying three vehicles belonging to a potential rival, Terence Sharkey. The case went to court but collapsed when two key witnesses mysteriously failed to appear. A former assistant told me that he had "helped take care of the matter". Sharkey's venture never recovered.

In that same year Gunter was also up before the judge for "sexually importuning for immoral purposes" on Hampstead Heath with Adil Demir, the son of a Turkish restaurant owner from Tottenham. He was given a minimal fine. In the macho world of the car business in an area dominated for a while by the brutal rule of the Kray brothers, it was by sheer force of personality, mainly through his camp appearance and exaggerated mannerisms, and sheer force period that Gunter largely escaped the underlying homophobia of the day. Nevertheless, despite his court case, which received little press coverage, he never publicly admitted his homosexuality even after the prejudicial laws towards it were repealed. It was a dichotomy that friends and employees initially found baffling especially as one of his favourite expressions was "I'd love him to ride on my pink 'un," which had little to do with his famous limousine. When news reached him that a business acquaintance, Harry Sheldon, had called him a "shirtlifter", Sheldon suffered serious facial injuries in a knife attack. He accused Gunter of being behind it but could find no proof. Again, when another acquaintance Paul Meredith described Gunter's business as a "poof's game", his house was set on fire. Again, no one was able to prove it at the time but friends of Gunter's admitted after his death that he was behind the attack. Those who worked for him loved the bonhomie, the risqué humour and his generosity. But few did not find him intimidating and several succumbed to his tendency to bear grudges. Gunter had many sexual partners throughout his life but in his last decade he lived on and off with a young Italian man Carlo Flagellati whom he met on the Ferrari stand at the Motor Show and who died two years ago from AIDS. However, there were persistent, though unsubstantiated rumours, that Gunter enjoyed more and more the company of young boys and taking them for a ride in his limousines involved more than mere sightseeing. No complaints were ever made, and it should be said that Gunter raised many millions of pounds over the years for a variety of charities.

Gunter's limo business went from strength to strength and stretched literally into the 1960s and 1970s. He catered for every celebrity passenger's individual tastes down to the particular label of champagne kept in the cocktail cabinet, to the make of chocolates, in the case it is rumoured of Robert Mitchum, the type of marijuana, and for various Hollywood lotharios their particular choice in men or women. He loved the limelight and photographs of him with Liberace, Diana Dors, Judy Garland and Fred Astaire adorned his office wall. His Christmas card list included many a movie star and he made regular trips to Las Vegas, a town that catered to his kitsch tastes. By the time of his retirement in 1997, Gunter had built up the business nationwide. His "pink 'un" or at least clones of the original car, would be just as likely gracing the parking lots of the Blackpool Winter Gardens, Aintree or the Bradford Alhambra, as it would be of Leicester Square or Covent Garden.

Eventually, as more and more firms aped his company, Gunter retired and the company was taken over by his brother Fred.

It was not to be a 'slippers and pipe' retirement. He joined his local Rochester amateur dramatic club where he appeared in several plays such as The Boys in the Band and Cabaret. He also "starred" as an extra in two episodes of The Bill, most famously being murdered in the first scene before re-appearing on a mortuary slab. He would live up to his initials GG by becoming a regular and colourful sight at the Kempton Park racecourse and entered into a three-part ownership of several, almost completely unsuccessful, racehorses together with a syndicate of friends that included a vet and a farrier "to keep the costs down" he said.

Gordon Gunter met his death while singing, in the company of his beloved Rochester Boy Scout group whom he was entertaining around a campfire in his garden. He collapsed during 'There's a Hole in my Bucket' and died during 'If You're Happy and You Know It'. He is survived by his brother Fred."

When the obituary hit the streets, Steve rang Mr Choudhury at the Hackney Messenger and gave him contact details of several people whom he was unable to persuade to come forward with more specific information about GG's liking for under-age boys.

19 REHEARSAL

"I see your friend Steve Graham has written about Gordon Gunter, that old crook with the pink limo."

Anthony Dukes was lounging at his desk peering at a copy of the National Herald. Ben turned to look at him. "Does he say he was a crook?"

"More or less. It seems like he wasn't averse to putting one over on his rivals not to mention a penchant for underage boys. Let's hope Mr Graham isn't sleeping with the fishes sometime soon."

"You know I've been thinking, obituaries are more than just a celebration of life, they tell us something about society too, about our views and our social mores," opined The Stick dreamily.

"Good God, the woman's taking this job too seriously," blustered Anthony.

The Stick continued unabashed.

"I mean cottaging. That's a phenomenon that people are already looking back on as a reaction to our proscriptive laws on homosexuality."

"Looking back? It's still going on," retorted Anthony.

"Well there's a part that says something about certain gay men," continued The Stick, "and there's a part that says something about the laws that discriminate against gay people of both sexes. I've read that obit too and that pink limo will undoubtedly say something about our social attitudes to someone reading that obit in a hundred years time."

"Very postmodernist," said Ben.

"Don't encourage her," Anthony interjected.

Ben continued equally determined and with a more serious look on his face.

"The people Steve chooses to write about says something about our society today. Until fairly recently, it was only the great and the good who got a newspaper send-off. And speaking of a hundred years ago, I remember reading the Times obit of Oscar Wilde and it concentrated mostly on his 'perverted' life rather than his literary attributes."

"Didn't realise you were that old, Ben," said Anthony.

The Stick looked at Ben to see if there would be any comeback to Anthony's last remark. When there wasn't, she continued with a glint in her eye.

"I was reading somewhere that for many years, before we women cast off the yoke of oppression from men like you, we were given obits because of the men we were married to, and lauded for being dutiful wives, affectionate, obedient, passive and all the rest. Then once we started taking part in public life on a large scale our obits finally mentioned our achievements."

Anthony smiled at Ben. Both were impressed by The Stick's knowledge of the subject and Ben took up her thread.

""You're absolutely right, Sticky, and obits can often say something about society as much by who they leave out as who they include. You mention women; they still get a lower share of obits as we know. But in past centuries you hardly see any from the ethnic minorities. Even with men the attributes listed in their obits changed when social values or circumstances altered. Take The Daily Telegraph's penchant for military men's obituaries. That's obviously because we'd had two World Wars for men to show their heroism. These people often did more in their war years than they did in the rest of their lives and it makes good reading. I suppose we've always had wars, so ample fodder for the obit columns but I read somewhere that during the industrial revolution, often military achievements gave way to business acumen and success."

"So now we're an all inclusive democratic society, so Steve Graham can write about car salesmen, bus conductors and the rest," concluded The Stick.

Anthony shifted slightly in his chair and put down his newspaper in order to contribute more fully to the discussion. "Is it that, or is it because there's such a circulation war going on out there that you've got to try something different?" he said.

"That too, no doubt," replied Ben.

"But it also perhaps shows how our rigid class system has broken down. Before it was all aristos and generals and now we let the hoi polloi in," added The Stick.

"We've still got a long way to go though," said Anthony. "I'm looking forward to the day when the Queen Mother's death would have been headlined on the local news, 'Centenarian's life of luxury comes to an end in Westminster. Taxpayers breathe sigh of relief'."

There was a certain irritation in Anthony's delivery that stemmed from the fact that he and his colleagues were taking part in a royal obit rehearsal. This was for him a futile exercise held a couple of times a year in which the news operation, under the leadership of the Head of News, swung into action under the assumption that a member of the royal family had died. Reporters were sent off to various parts of the building to pretend that they were at Windsor Castle or Balmoral and interviewers would have to ask them all sorts of questions that they were ordered to answer with a straight face. It was futile because when the real event had taken place when the Queen Mother died, the editorial staff had lost their heads, thrown out all the lessons learned in decades of rehearsals and treated it like it was a surprise news story in the same way as Diana's death had been. The two could not have been more different.

"Social attitudes to the royals have ebbed and flowed in the short time I've been in this job," said Ben.

"When I first came here I remember the BBC went through a phase of wanting nothing much to do with the Royals. They would always follow The Queen on every foreign tour, then they started to ignore them. ITV then had the sense to realise you could make loads of money packaging foreign tours for sale to overseas broadcasters. Of course, then Diana came along and everything changed."

"How come Keith isn't here?" asked Anthony. "Has he got some kind of royal pardon or is he out on the golf course playing real golf and hitting his ball into real lakes?"

"He's down seeing the old Bill today about his car and Carla's fiancé," answered Ben. "We've copied the footage so that they can see it for themselves. I had to get permission from them upstairs and Jon, our intrepid crime correspondent's gone with him."

"So the crime correspondent's got off the rehearsal too, eh. What a surprise! Being here's a bloody crime, bloody royal wasters."

"Wasters or not, they keep us in work."

"What do you reckon about old Keith, eh?" Anthony smirked. "I reckon he's in on it with Carla's fiancé. Making a bit of money on the side."

"That's not funny," protested The Stick indignantly.

"If Keith had tried to shoot Carla Wilson he'd have probably shot himself by mistake," added Ben. "Come on people, I'm cracking the whip."

"Knowing that my death day was being rehearsed would make my knees tremble," said The Stick.

"If your knees trembled, they'd sound like fucking castanets," said Anthony The Stick raised two fingers in his direction.

20 MEDLOCK

Detective Chief Inspector Susan Medlock of Scotland Yard finished re-reading Gordon Gunter's obituary in the *National Herald* and tossed the newspaper on to her metal office desk, finding a space between the numerous files and papers scattered untidily upon it. Slowly she diverted her gaze towards her fifth floor window, and in a moment or two of contemplation widened the space between two sections of the Venetian blind with her thumb and forefinger to reveal the busy urban street below. There was a line in the obituary that had set her thinking, that had given her a possible lead and she was excited by it in her downbeat way. She was feeling a little better about life in general, or more specifically about her career, which given the absurd number of hours she spent on police business, amounted to much the same thing. She was in her late thirties and single. She wasn't exactly proud of her marital status or her non-marital status as she called it. However, she had seen so many of her fellow female colleagues' career progression hindered by family commitments in an organisation that was institutionally male oriented. She had decided therefore that marriage was not high on her list of priorities, especially since the notion of having children did not appeal. It was a decision influenced by the men with whom she had forged relationships who had more or less given up on her when they came to realise that they would always play second fiddle to her job even when she was a lowly constable. The only people who understood the kind of experiences she had to endure, and these ranged from the sight of gruesome stabbings at murder scenes to the ugly back-stabbings in the politics of the Met, were fellow police officers. They knew the language – the way life worked in the police world. But the last people she wanted to establish relationships outside of work were policemen. She was determined that one day she would rise to the level of Chief Constable and no one, not least children of her own, would stand in her way. The battles on her way up the greasy pole had been hard fought and would doubtless become bloodier but she possessed an inner strength that her parents had often remarked upon and which they always claimed they had spotted at an early age.

"Susan always had stickability," her mother was wont to say. "You could blindfold her, spin her round a dozen times and she'd always choose the right path and see it through to the end."

DCI Medlock was feeling better about life because she and her team had achieved a breakthrough in one of the two major investigations she was leading, the Irina Lockyer case. She was always confident this would happen but progress had been painstakingly slow as her bosses together with sections of the media and, indirectly, certain members of parliament, were not so slow in reminding her. Part of the problem was that it had taken time for the Nigerian girls who had escaped the clutches of the Albanian sex-traffickers to recover from the trauma of the murder attempt upon them and the perceived accidental killing of Irina. They remained in constant fear that their former slave masters would try again despite police protection. Gradually however, their reticence to provide a full picture of their captors was overcome. A stakeout of the premises in which they held their captives had at last resulted in the arrests of some of the main figures that the two girls positively identified. It was a small victory in a war that was too often beset with defeats. Privately, Medlock was bitterly upset that successive governments had failed to grapple properly with the issue and had lobbied as many people as she could to keep the matter alive in the political arena, and it was the knowledge that she was limited in this regard by her relatively low status as a DCI that was another spur to her ambitions to further herself.

However, it was the Carla Wilson murder that had inflicted upon her the bigger headache. After endless speculation – gangland murder, robbery, trophy killing - there had been a major development. She had sent in the heavies when a tip-off from a member of the public had alerted her team to the identity of a man whom Wilson had reported as having been bothering her only two weeks before her murder. They broke into his flat and uncovered a shrine to the murdered broadcaster; pictures all over each wall, childlike poems to her in scrapbooks, newspaper and magazine cuttings scattered everywhere and several books she had either written or collaborated on piled on the floor. It was a textbook cliché as befitted its tenant: loner, learning difficulties, history of mental problems. The DCI's bosses were both ecstatic and relieved. After the 'T's were crossed and the 'I's dotted it would be done and dusted, in the can. Except it wasn't. As yet she had found no evidence to link the suspect with Carla's murder. He had an alibi, it may be false; there were no forensics, he may just have been careful; there was no motive, he professed to love her. But she was engaged. Could jealousy be enough to swing his unstable mind? Maybe, but his psychiatrist said he had no violent traits. But psychiatrists are all nutters, aren't they? That Carla had been filming a series about street gangs was the first and obvious lead. But there again, there was nothing to go on. Exhaustive inquiries had unearthed not a single piece of evidence. Then a small but possibly significant detail had found itself on a post-it note left on her desk. Carla's fiancé had been filmed getting into a car that was not only stolen but could be the same one seen at the murder of Irina. Could the two murders be linked? It was almost too good to be true. And that was what worried her. Her telephone rang. A voice said, "Mr Graham has arrived, Guv."

Steve entered the room and gave DCI Medlock a rueful smile. He was about to ask her the reason for his summons when he noticed his obituary of Gordon Gunter on her desk.

"Ah, I see you have superior reading tastes DCI Medlock. Didn't see you as a Herald reader, let alone an afficianado of the obituary."

DCI Medlock remained dead-pan, paused and then spoke quietly, anxious to either confirm or dispel a notion that was forefront in her mind. "What's your game, Mr Graham?" Steve was momentarily taken aback.

"It purports to be journalism, inspector though others may refer to it as...."

"Less of your smart-aleck remarks. What I mean is what's going on with you obituary writers?"

"I really don't know to what you are referring, DCI Medlock."

Medlock thumped the table. "What I'm referring to is first you're found to have been outside a house a couple of days before a murder takes place. It turns out you know the victim. Then one of your obituary friends comes to collect you, then another tells us that the car you saw that day is actually his. Is this some sort of silly game, some pathetic wind up? Because if it is you could be in serious trouble Mr Graham."

DCI Medlock prided herself on being able to sniff a lie from 20 paces. When she saw Steve's face transform instantly from superciliousness to perplexity she guessed it was genuine. Steve had known nothing about Keith's stolen car. He didn't know Keith and was as surprised as DCI Medlock had been when there appeared to be a link. DCI Medlock opened a file on her desk and brought out a picture of Keith's car.

"Is this the vehicle you saw that day?"

Steve looked carefully at it, saw the SG in the licence plate and nodded his head.

"Yes, this is it. It's the same colour and of course the registration, my initials. But there's another thing that I now remember, the paintwork on the front. It's either a bodged job or a poor example of abstract expressionism. I guess the former. Yes, this is the car I saw, definitely."

He'd mouthed the words she was hoping for. A whole new line of enquiry, a sensational one at that, was opening up.

"Have I passed the test? Do I win the two week holiday in the Turks and Cacos Islands?" Medlock remained poker-faced and produced a brown envelope from her desk drawer from which she removed four photographs.

"I want you to look at these faces and tell me if you recognise any of them." She passed him the first one.

" Christ, this is no beauty contest. This guy must be guilty because only a guilty person could be this ugly. Never seen him before." Medlock took the photo back and passed him the next one.

"God, and I thought the other guy was ugly! This bloke should audition for Treasure Island. All he needs is an eye-patch. No, don't recognise him." Beneath her deadpan look, Medlock was disappointed. She gave him number three.

"Ah yes, well we've all seen Carla Wilson's fiancé and before you ask, no I don't remember him being in the car. I only saw one person for a few seconds and it wasn't him. Do you suspect him then?"

"I might as well tell you as you'll find out anyway, that he was seen getting into the blue BMW vehicle that you've identified. "

"Really!" Steve's reaction struck Medlock as being one of genuine surprise. The journalist was practically salivating over the desk.

"So he could be mixed up in all this? Shiver my fucking timbers. Have you arrested him?"

"Not yet, he appears to have flown the coop."

"So my friend Ben knows about this presumably? I wonder why he didn't tell me."

Medlock knew the answer: it was simply that Steve had not informed Ben about the SG initials and he hadn't therefore made the connection. As Steve got up to go, anxious to let his crime desk know of the development, DCI Medlock gestured for him to wait.

"There's one more picture for you to see." She passed it to him. His surprise when he looked at it signalled that she had hit the jackpot.

"Fuck me, this is the bloke that kissed me. Would you believe it?"

Medlock was inwardly thrilled at Steve's recognition but taken aback at the detail.

"This is one of Gordon Gunter's guys. " Steve stared at the photograph. Eventually Medlock broke the pregnant silence.

"Don't tell me that he kissed you on Hampstead Heath?"

Steve looked up from the photo, and stared at her before smiling and adding, "No, on the fucking lips." DCI Medlock was more relieved than amused when Steve explained the circumstances of the anything-but-amorous nature of his encounter with the man he remembered as being called Alan. The police had identified this man as having consorted with the Albanian gang. Her team had long suspected that Gordon Gunter had been involved in supplying prostitutes to the rich and famous. She could see that Steve had been told as much and had mentioned it in his obituary. Now they had a positive indication that the Albanian gang had been renting out their girls to Gunter for his clients to use. What's more, these obituarists had also provided a link between Carla Wilson's fiancé and the Albanians. Her misgivings about the charges placed against the loner they had arrested were borne out. There was another reason for her relief at the circumstances surrounding the kiss. She would have been instinctively disappointed if Steve had been gay because, beneath her crusty exterior, DCI Medlock, though she would never admit it to herself, had found both his looks and his personality strangely appealing. She found that beneath the faux arrogance was someone whose sense of humour chimed with hers. She questioned Steve for a further hour to grill him on all he knew about Gunter's involvement with under-age boys and about this Alan fellow. Then she released him so that he could convey the developments to his newspaper. However, she noticed a gradual change in his attitude and demeanour during this period. She felt Steve's excitement and pleasure at being able to help account for missing pieces in the jigsaw of two high-profile crimes dissipate at the realisation that the threat to his own security may well have increased. The Albanians had already shown how ruthless they could be; perhaps now Gordon Gunter's brother Fred who'd taken exception to his brother's obituary might be in league with them and want Steve dead. That she was unable to calm his fears only made both feel worse. Steve was to feel worse still later that same day.

21 ALBIE

Steve emerged slowly from the front door of a small hotel near Victoria Station. The dying light helped obscure the tears that had welled up as he walked away. He gave a final glance behind him at the window that reflected the flickering light from a yellow AA sign. Both the sign and the hotel it was endorsing had seen better days. There was no one at the window. With thoughts in his head racing round with centrifugal force, he headed towards the underground station. It was raining slightly but for all he cared the heavens could have been pouring buckets upon him and him alone. He paused and fished inside his pocket for a cigarette. He'd cut down heavily on his habit but couldn't resist in times of stress. As he flicked the lighter, his mind was suddenly jarred into sharp focus by the sight of none other than the Hairy Wart sidling by on the other side of the street, illuminated by a bright street lamp. It was instant recognition: the blemish, the gait, and the same yellow anorak. If there was any doubt at all, it was banished when he shouted at him only to see The Wart immediately take off down the street. This was too much for Steve in his heightened state of mind. Without hesitation, he threw away his cigarette and in a devil-may-care attitude, gave chase. It didn't last long. The Hairy Wart soon disappeared behind a phalanx of car headlights. "Why are you following me?" muttered Steve to himself with a desperation bordering on despair. He wondered to himself why, if this was an Albanian or Cockney hit man, didn't he strike? The opportunity in a dark side street would have been ideal with so few people about. Perhaps he was just being cautious, a professional wanting to execute his task in the perfect way, with no witnesses. On the other hand, why choose someone to be an assassin with such an obvious identifiable facial mark? In a whirlwind state of confusion, Steve walked into the entrance to the Tube, sat on the black and white tiled floor, leant against a wall and feeling very sorry for himself lit another cigarette, caring not a jot for the stares he received from passing commuters. After a few minutes, one of those passers-by turned out to be none other than Hilary on her way to catching the evening train home. Aghast, she looked down and asked, “Steve, what on earth are you doing down there? You look like a down and out beggar.” Steve paused to take in a last drag from his cigarette before answering, “I was waiting for you, Hilary.” Hilary looked around her in the hope that no one she knew would see her conversing with this seeming reprobate. She would have proffered her hand to help him to his feet but, at half his size, he would have brought her down to his level in more ways than one.

“Are you catching the train?”

"Yep”

“Come on then.”

Steve stood up and the pair went through the barrier and made their way down the escalator towards the platform. Once on board, he began telling Hilary how he had received an abusive call from Gordon Gunter’s brother about his reference to young boys in his obituary and that he had “outed” his brother. “Where was the fuckin’ respect?” the brother had asked. No manner of suggesting that everyone knew of his homosexuality anyway and that his court case was in the public domain made any difference to the brother’s view that, for whatever reason Gordon had never declared himself gay in public while he was alive and that Steve had therefore no right to do so when he was dead. Gordon’s brother had expressed his views in somewhat simpler and more threatening terms. Though Hilary had always regarded Steve as being disregardful of family sensitivities, she offered her sympathy to something that had clearly upset him. Hilary had never seen him so fraught.

“So what were you doing in Victoria and why were you looking so downbeat?” Hilary enquired again. “And don’t say you were waiting for me.”

“I was meeting an old friend who I hadn’t seen for years but then I saw the Hairy Wart.”

Though Steve's answer was true, it obscured the real significance of his meeting. Hilary had had no idea that Steve was being followed and shared his concern. She asked what Maria thought of it all. His reply was that she seemed to think it was a figment of his overactive imagination and that stress was getting the better of him. Hilary told Steve, above the clatter of the tube carriage, that she too would be panicking if she thought that she was being followed. There was something though about his description of his pursuer that rang a bell somewhere in her mind, a notion that she may have seen this man before. As she couldn't be certain, she didn't mention it.

As they resurfaced and joined the throng headed for the overground train, they met Ben. The three flashed their season tickets to the staff member on duty. Hilary was glad it wasn't The Ogre. Doubtless Steve would have been unable to stifle a comment in the mood he was in. The three boarded a carriage that was already fast filling up with passengers. However, Hilary immediately spotted three vacant seats, the last ones left, two of which were together, the other on its own. She quickened her pace and grabbed one of the two and Ben who was following her, sat in the one next to her. Steve was about to sit in the only other vacant seat on the other side of the aisle next to a man he knew vaguely as Zachariah. There had been a residual animosity between Steve and Zachariah in the past. Zachariah always liked to sit next to his wife Sheila when he travelled home. The problem was that since Sheila and he did not work together, they did not arrive at the train at precisely the same times. This usually was of no consequence since as long as there were spare seats they could normally find two together, sometimes after some musical chairs with other passengers. A problem arose when the train was full, however. Zachariah had developed a procedure whereby he "guarded" the seat for Sheila even though she hadn't yet arrived thereby depriving someone who had turned up before Sheila of a place to sit. Zachariah had acquired a certain notoriety for this practice and though Steve had never until now been the unlucky victim of Zac's proprietal instincts, he had nevertheless exchanged angry words with him about it. The words “arrogant little bastard” had been directed towards Zachariah and he became known among Steve’s band of commuter buddies as “ALB” then “Albie”. On this occasion Albie had placed a rucksack on the vacant seat next to the window. If Steve were to take it he would have to push past him, and since Albie was a rather stocky individual, negotiation would be necessary. The problem for both parties though was that Steve was in no mood for negotiating something that he felt was non-negotiable.

“Is that seat free, Zachariah?”

“No, it’s Sheila’s.”

"Is Sheila here?”

"Yes, she’s coming.”

“You mean she isn’t here.”

"I said she’s coming.”

"I heard what you said and since she isn’t here I’m asking you politely to give up that seat.”

Albie sat there without looking at Steve and refusing to discuss the matter further.

“I’ll say it again, impolitely, Zachariah, I want that fucking seat.” One or two passengers glanced at the pair. Albie again refused to look Steve in the eye, neither gracing him with a reply.

“Look, you piece of putrid shit, I’ll say this one more time, are you going to give me that seat?”

“One more time or what?” said Zachariah slowly rising to his feet and at last making eye contact.

Hilary experienced a sense of foreboding as soon as she saw the confrontation develop. But even in his state, she hadn’t expected such a reaction. The sound of Steve’s knuckle connecting with Zachariah’s cheekbone managed to pierce the general hubbub of the carriage stopping everyone in their tracks even before the ensuing mayhem. It had much more of a crack to it than the sound effect of a punch so familiar from television and the movies.

There's nothing like a potent mixture of adrenaline and testosterone in a sleepy railway carriage to cause a stir. After a short exchange of fisticuffs, the two combatants wrestled with each other as Steve tried to oust Albie's corpulent frame from his seat. At one time, Albie managed to pin Steve's head against the window much to the consternation of passers-by on the platform. Women, including Hilary, shouted for the pair to stop. In the meantime, several male passengers attempted to pull the two rutting stags apart though not before several more blows were exchanged. Sheila's arrival on the scene did not aid matters as she began raining blows upon Steve's back with her fists while screaming abuse. Hilary and another woman attempted to pull her back. There was more screaming and shouting as hair was pulled. Sheila kicked out before swinging her bag round narrowly passing over Hilary's head, swearing as she did so. Her mobile phone flew out of the bag, cracked against a window and began playing the theme tune to Monty Python. Another woman appeared from nowhere and whacked Steve over the head with an umbrella. He turned around and saw that it was Mrs Shithouse exacting revenge. The flurry of activity and the cacophony of sound became the focus of both outrage and amusement from other passengers. Eventually, before a rail official could intervene, Ben hauled Steve away from the fracas and shepherded him out of the carriage as Albie and Sheila continued their torrent of bad language in Steve's direction. The whole shebang lasted barely a couple of minutes, though as Hilary later informed them, it was still being talked about in the carriage half an hour later. Sheila got her seat.

"What on earth were you thinking of, Steve? That bloke's not worth the steam off your piss."

No matter how much Ben tried to make sense of it, Steve was not to be subdued. Shaking with rage, he twice tried to return to the carriage to “finish the bastard off” only for Ben to pull him back. It was not until they reached a nearby pub that Steve calmed down with the aid of a large brandy. Once more, as Ben again asked him why he had reacted so, Steve’s eyes began to water.

“He was just the last straw. I’ve had one of those days, Ben.”

Ben nodded but said nothing, waiting for Steve to elaborate.

“I feel my life’s like being on the train but that it’s going out of control. It’s like it gets to my station but doesn’t stop. I know you’ll think I’m being paranoid but I saw the Hairy Wart again. He seems to be toying with me. The police say they can do nothing and I feel absolutely vulnerable. I even chased him today, and the police say if he was trying to kill me he wouldn’t run away. But if he’s not then who is he? Maybe he’s not trying to kill me, maybe he’s just trying to intimidate me, I just don’t know.” Ben shrugged his shoulders. Both sipped their drinks and after a short pause Ben continued. “You know Albie might press charges for assault.”

“Let him, the little bastard.”

”Pity you didn’t think about it before you hit him.”

Steve looked crestfallen. “That guy was waiting to be hit. I swear if I hadn’t done it, someone else would have sooner or later.”

”But it has to be you, doesn’t it Steve. You put yourself in the firing line.”

”You mean I stand up for what’s right?”

“There has to be better ways of standing up for what’s right.”

Steve gave a resigned look, a pained expression. “I’m an impulsive sort of character, Ben. I don’t look for trouble but if I see injustice at whatever level it upsets me.”

“There are injustices happening every day everywhere. You have to prioritise. Albie’s behaviour is arrogant but he’s not worth having to be punished for. He isn’t worth hitting is what I’m trying to say.”

Steve took another sip of brandy. “It was a lovely punch, though. Muhammad Ali would have been proud of that one.”

"I didn’t see it but you’re missing the point.”

“Yes, all right, I shouldn’t have done it, I know.”

Steve gulped the last of his drink, before exhaling strongly and looking Ben square in the eye.

“There’s something I want you to do for me, Ben.” Steve reached into the breast pocket of his jacket and took out a sealed brown envelope.

“Would you hang on to this for a while, just in case something happens to me. I’ll take it back as soon as all this blows over, if it does blow over.”

"Of course it’s going to blow over.” Steve passed the envelope to Ben who looked perplexed.

“Can I ask what’s in it?”

“No you can’t but don’t worry it’s nothing incriminating or underhand, no drugs or anything.”

“Glad to hear it.” Ben looked uncomfortable nevertheless despite Steve’s reassurance.

“Don’t worry Ben, it’s quite harmless. I just don’t want it falling into the wrong hands in case anything happens to me, believe me.”

“All right but I’m sure nothing’s going to happen to you in that way.” Ben placed the envelope into his inside coat pocket and the pair decided it was time to leave. Ben knocked back his drink and they left to catch the next train. They arrived in good time with plenty of spare seats, a relief to both of them. Ben suggested that perhaps the one way to avoid being taken to court was to apologise to Albie. The very thought of it caused Steve's blood pressure to rise but as the journey progressed he began to see the sense of the idea albeit with huge reluctance. More weight was added to the suggestion when Ben took a call from Hilary who informed him that she and others had persuaded an irate Albie to sleep on the notion of going through with an assault charge until the morning, so buying Steve a little time. If Steve thought the ructions of the day had passed, he was mistaken. When he arrived home he told Maria what had occurred on the train and felt the full force of her reprimands. The slow burn of antagonism over the past months suddenly exploded. The catalyst was none other than the Hairy Wart. When Steve admitted how much this menace was affecting him, Maria stunned him by coming clean. She confessed that the Hairy Wart was none other than one of her father's employees whom he had hired to keep tabs on Steve's whereabouts since he suspected him of being unfaithful to his daughter. Steve could not believe what he was hearing. In earlier days crockery might have been thrown, but the recriminations that flew from both quarters were more hurtful.

"I can't believe you could be complicit in such a scheme of deceit," screamed Steve thumping the kitchen table. "You knew how much stress it was causing me yet you allowed it to carry on."

"I let it carry on because I believed you were carrying on, carrying on with someone else," was the even shriller reply.

"I've told you I don't know how many times that I'm not carrying on with anybody."

"Then where were you the night before you were arrested? And who were you seeing in Victoria this evening?"

"My goodness, doesn't news travel fast! I told you that I was away on a job on the night before I was arrested and as for tonight I was visiting an old friend who contacted me out of the blue who was in London and we had a quick drink. I didn't tell you because you didn't know that person. I mean how do I know that you haven't been carrying on with the butcher, the baker and the candlestick maker while I'm at work? Is this where our so-called marriage has got to when every time I visit someone I'm having an affair with them?"

And so the arguments went back and forth, insult heaped upon insult, accusation followed by counter accusation. Finally, after tears from both sides there was the kind of reconciliation borne out of weariness as with two boxers who had fought each other to a standstill. By two in the morning a truce had been called and each retired to their respective corners, in this instance separate bedrooms. When Steve's phone alarm let forth its irritatingly jolly techno jingle at seven o'clock the following morning, all quality sleep had been denied him thanks to the disparate thoughts that had cascaded through his mind most of the night.

22 RED SIGNAL

The watery autumnal sun glorified every shade of colour in the surrounding trees that even Steve in his half-deadened, sleep-deprived state found breath taking.

"Don't run too far ahead, William," he shouted as his son, oversized satchel on his shoulder, chased a cat for a few metres before it disappeared into a hedgerow.

"What were you and Mummy arguing about last night?" asked Naomi, walking by his side.

"We were just having a disagreement about something, "he replied softly.

"I don't like it when you argue," she said, stern-faced.

"We don't like it either," he muttered.

"So why do you do it?"

This was an awkward conversation that Steve could have done without given his fragile physical and emotional state but Naomi deserved an answer.

"Well sometimes you just get so worked up about something that you can't help it. Do you remember when you had an argument with Adebola in the playground last week? It was a bit like that."

"Adebola was being really stupid. She called me a cow."

"Why?" asked Steve desperate to shift the focus away from him and Maria.

"Because she said I stole her comb but It was mine anyway."

"Well you should have told her that cows don't need combs because they don't have any hair to comb and, besides, they don't have any hands to hold the comb with."

"Don't be silly, Daddy."

A little further along the way to school she asked, "Are you and Mummy getting divorced?"

"Of course we're not. It was only an argument. You're still going to Adebola's party on Saturday aren't you?"

"Yes."

"There, you see, you can still be friends with people you argue with. By the way, have you bought her a present yet?"

"Yes"

"What have you bought her?"

"A comb," said Naomi bursting out laughing.

Steve laughed too and William came back to find out what the joke was all about.

After dropping his kids off at the school gate and exchanging pleasantries with one or two of the mothers he recognised, Steve decided that rather than go home to fetch the car, he would walk the two miles to the station. He phoned Maria to tell her she could use the car. The spectacle of autumnal beauty was enough to transcend his weariness and the fact that he knew that the Hairy Wart was not an Albanian assassin was a weight off his mind. Besides, he had other matters to think about. The fact that he hadn't had a policeman knocking at his door at some unearthly hour suggested that Albie had heeded Hilary's counsel and had not reported yesterday's incident, at least not yet. He would have to make a pre-emptive move. There were other serious matters worrying him, among them a woman in Victoria. As he turned the final corner to the station approach, the sight of Ben once more cursing at his bicycle lifted his mood. He'd managed to entangle his left trouser leg in the chain resulting in both a rip and a greasy stain. Given the support Ben had lent him the previous evening, Steve's ribbing was milder than it might have been. The two of them walked on to the platform where Hilary was already waiting. Steve sneaked up behind her and gave her a bear hug. She turned round and looked up at him.

"Steve, there's a guy who works at the tyre place on Grosvenor Road, you know where St James primary school is, he's got a hairy thing on his face. You remember I was telling you that somewhere in my mind I thought I knew I'd seen someone like that. Maybe it's him."

"Don't worry Hilary, that's sorted. It's nothing to worry about after all."

"Really?" said Ben looking puzzled.

"Yes, it was all a misunderstanding, someone who works with Maria's father."

"Very mysterious," said Hilary.

Having dealt with that issue rather perfunctorily, once more Steve changed the subject to avoid any further interrogation. "More to the point, Hilary, have you seen Albie?"

"No, sorry. I texted Robbie who's on the earlier train that Albie normally takes but he hasn't seen him either."

Steve was worried by this news. He was hoping to have an apologetic word with Albie though doubtless Albie would shun him.

"I'm going to have to find out where this bloke lives or works but nobody's contacted me about it so I may have you to thank for that, Hilary."

"Well don't do it again, for Christ's sake," she replied. "My efforts on your behalf do not stretch too far."

“Thanks anyway,” said Steve with genuine gratitude.

When the train eventually arrived, some 10 minutes or so late, Steve took a seat separate from his friends explaining that he was going to try and grab forty winks on the journey seeing as he’d achieved very few overnight. However, before he sat down, several commuters with whom he shared a nodding acquaintance complimented him on his pugilistic acumen especially against one so obviously disliked. He had to disassociate himself with one suggestion though, that he “should have clocked his bird and all”. One rather sniffy woman in her sixties wearing what resembled an Alpine hunting hat accused Steve and Zachariah of behaving like hooligans. Steve pacified her a little by admitting that he regretted what he’d done and apologised to her. None of those he spoke to had any contact details for Albie with the exception of one man who knew that he sometimes served in the Nag’s Head pub in the evenings, a detail for which Steve was very grateful. In the meantime, the train had come to a standstill and the click of the tannoy presaged the usual excuse.

“This is your driver speaking. Due to unforeseen circumstances there’ll be a short delay. Sorry for any inconvenience.”

Once separated from Steve, Hilary eschewed her book in favour of probing Ben on what Steve meant about Hairy Wart and what he might have been doing in Victoria when she discovered him sitting in the tube station. Ben pleaded genuine ignorance to both these matters. Hilary and Ben both agreed that they’d never seen Steve in quite such a conciliatory and submissive mood, as he was this morning. Both admitted too though that in general they’d never seen him so stressed.

“This is your driver speaking again. We’re still delayed I’m afraid. Sorry for the inconvenience. I expect it’s due to leaves on the line.”

There were murmurs of discontent around the carriage. Phones were taken out and excuses for projected lateness were made. Ben turned round to look at Steve who had fallen asleep. Hilary and Ben then began speculating as to whether or not Steve might face charges as a result of yesterday's fisticuffs.

"Ladies and gentlemen, this is your driver again. There doesn't appear to be any more movement at the moment. Nobody's telling me why. Maybe the women who sweep the leaves away as we go along have taken ill. Like you, I'm just sitting here doing the crossword. Anyone know any animals from the cat family beginning with o, six letters?" Ben was of the opinion that Albie might be persuaded not to prosecute since Sheila was behaving very aggressively and could perhaps be indicted too. Maybe there was a case for a quid pro quo here. Hilary wasn't so sure. Their conversation was interrupted once more.

"Ladies and gentlemen, this is your driver speaking again. Seems I was right what I said earlier. It is indeed leaves on the line that's causing the back-up. I keep telling them to abolish autumn or introduce a defoliation programme but they won't listen. Hello? We're moving. Oh, and the clue answer was ocelot."

At that, to the general bemusement of everyone bar Steve who was still sound asleep, the train jerked into movement. Having just recovered from the eccentric behaviour of the driver, another old friend weighed in.

"DOES HE HAVE BLOOD IN HIS STOOL?" The laughter outweighed the groans. As the journey progressed with no further delays, The Nurse continued in full flight dispensing her common sense remedies on her phone.

"I suggest all that's required are suppositories, dear, available from all leading chemists." Hilary looked at Steve. He was still asleep. Respite for a troubled soul, she thought. At this moment, as the train was approaching its penultimate stop, a young man of about 18 years pulled his rucksack from the rack above the table at which Ben, Hilary and two others sat. As he brought it down, a packet of condoms spilled from one of its pockets on to Ben's lap. The lad turned the colour of a ripe Victoria plum, apologised profusely and stuffed the prophylactics back into his bag. Hilary glanced at Ben and stifled a giggle while Ben looked wistfully at the youth and suggested that he take precautions against this eventuality repeating itself. The youth was too embarrassed to smile at this laboured pun. Hilary gazed at the picturesque rural scene visible from her window. The cloudless sky struck a vivid contrast with the faded yellow of a recently harvested field of grain. In the foreground a small stream sparkled and to her right she could see the tower of the old village church around which a flock of houses stood as if basking in the Lord's protection. Hilary imagined the view as having changed little in a hundred years or more, for there on the left a road wound up a hill to a large stately home. Here could live the patrician landowner, the man to whom the community owed their labour, their tithes, their livelihood. As the train began slowing on its approach to the next station, Hilary suddenly caught sight of a fox emerging from a clump of trees and pausing as if to capture in its fur the warmth of the sun. It turned towards the train momentarily, and in a seemingly arrogant fashion, raised its pointed nose and sniffed the air before trotting back behind the hedgerow, its sleek brown and white tail gradually disappearing from view. As Hilary turned towards Ben to share her excitement, and as the train door opened, a hooded figure moved swiftly like a shadow past Ben. There was a flash of metal before the person slipped through the door just before it closed. A sharp cry was followed by a scream. Hilary's face, still smiling from the gentle bucolic scene she had just enjoyed, metamorphosed into a picture of horror as she looked at Steve. There was a collective gasp. Hilary clasped both hands to her mouth. By the time Ben turned round, the blood that seeped from a stab wound had already formed a patch on Steve's white shirt the size of a tennis ball. Within a few seconds all traces of whiteness had been expunged. The woman who sat closest to Steve was in a state of hysteria and pointing to the door. She was trying to tell people that the assailant had escaped from the train but in her anxiety she was making little sense.

"Help him someone, help him, he's bleeding to death," cried an elderly man, unable to get near the scene of the crime. Someone pulled the emergency cord even though the train remained at the station. Several others called the emergency services. Panic ensued as people came to realise what had occurred. Then, piercing the tumult came the cry, "I'm a nurse, let me through." Passengers moved aside like Moses parting the Dead Sea. Taking one look at Steve's predicament The Nurse cried, "Tissues, anyone got tissues." Two people close by obliged and she knelt down to attempt to staunch the bleeding. Steve was still conscious and completely still. Ben, whose face had turned almost as pale as Steve's, knelt down next to The Nurse to offer assistance though he had never felt so helpless in his life. Steve was beginning to lose consciousness and with a semi-vacant expression looked at The Nurse and uttered a few words, his last words. The Nurse did her best to locate the wound but it was soon apparent that there was nothing she could do. Her suspicions, correct as it turned out, were that Steve had been stabbed through the heart. Two rail workers arrived and opened the door to the carriage that despite being quite crowded had developed an almost reverent quiet in which even the sobbing seemed gentle. The rail workers would have allowed people to disembark but once they were told what had happened decided that it was best if people stayed put until the police came. Eventually, the voice of tannoy man appeared. "Ladies and gentlemen, this train is being taken out of service owing to a mishap in one of the carriages. However, we ask you to remain where you are while we await instructions from the police." The police arrived some five minutes later, followed closely by an ambulance. The train was declared a crime scene, photographs were taken, Steve's corpse was eventually removed and it wasn't until several hours later that the train was shunted into a siding and the disruption to the rail service ended.

Ben, still shaking, called the news desk to inform them of what had happened. When the woman on duty said, "But there's been nothing on the wires," Ben nearly exploded. "Of course there's nothing on the wires, it's only just happened and I was on the train." All the anger, the frustration, fear and grief seemed to converge and he cut the call off. Later, when he'd calmed down, he called a colleague from the home desk, told him what had happened and to whom, and told him to embargo the name since his family would not yet have been informed. He then rang his office and The Stick answered.

"Hello, obits."

"Oh, hello Stick, is Anthony there?"

"No he's not, why what's wrong?"

The Stick had immediately sensed a tremor in his voice that she hadn't encountered before.

"I need to speak to him urgently, Stick. I've just witnessed a friend of mine being murdered on a train, Steve Graham."

The Stick let forth a gasp. "Oh My God," she cried and burst into tears. The last thing Ben wanted was to have to console someone when it was he that needed comforting so he asked her to give Anthony the message that he wanted to speak to him urgently. Anthony rang back a few minutes later and expressed his shock and his sympathy. Ben instructed him to prepare an obit on Steve, which could be published as soon as his name was released and Ben talked him through it, emphasising the common person nature of his obits, how popular an item they had become for the Herald and his latter connection with the Irina case. In the meantime, the police converted one of the waiting areas into an incident room, and Ben and Hilary who had been comforting one another as best they could, were eventually summoned. Neither was able to give an adequate description of the suspect in the hoodie and both explained about the fight with Zachariah and it was clear from the interviewing officer's reaction that several others had done the same. However, when both Ben and Hilary mentioned that Steve had been involved in the business with Irina and had been fearful of an attack by Albanian gangsters, the detectives became animated. When the officer asked Ben if he'd heard Steve's last words, he hesitated. The officer asked him to confirm what The Nurse had told them that she believed he'd said, "I've got no idea," that she took to mean a reference to the identity of his attacker. In fact, Ben could have sworn that Steve had looked at The Nurse and said, "I've got diarrhoea" but when he heard what The Nurse had quoted he thought it was best to concur and so he nodded in agreement. The police officer explained that they believed the attacker had been hiding in the toilet and had escaped through a fence beyond the station platform. They would be examining CCTV pictures as soon as was possible. Everything was noted, statements taken and Ben and Hilary who by now were physically and emotionally depleted, returned to the bosom of their respective families. And it wasn't even lunchtime.

Elizabeth picked Ben up from the station and consoled him as best she could. As she drove him home, Ben looked up at the sky. What a beautiful day on which to die, he thought. If Ben needed quiet and solitude, it wasn't his day, beautiful or not. His phone would not stop ringing. Every news channel, daily newspaper and news agency wanted to speak to him. It seemed that the Irina affair, which had highlighted Steve's profession, and the paradox of an obituary writer being killed, had caught the eye of news editors both at home and abroad. Ben couldn't turn his phone off because he was expecting more information from the police. He fielded only calls from his own organisation, giving quotes to colleagues on what he had witnessed. For the rest he asked Elizabeth to deal with by saying her husband was too upset to talk. However, by mid-afternoon several reporters began knocking on his door much to his annoyance. But since the events that had occurred continued to swirl around in his head so that he couldn't sleep anyway, Ben wrote a few lines about what he'd seen and about Steve in general, which he then read out to the assembled media and emailed to the Press Association. When DCI Medlock rang insisting on speaking to him, Elizabeth had to relent. She asked if he knew the whereabouts of Zachariah or any other information that might help them with their enquiries.

"I've told everything I know in my statement," he insisted. "But if I can think of anything else, you'll be the first to know," he said before ringing off.

It wasn't long before he learned of something else thanks indirectly to a phone call he received much later in the day. It was from Harry Fearnley, Steve's line manager at the Herald. After offering his genuine condolences and his gratitude for Ben's speaking to him, Fearnley told of how shocked they all were at the paper. There was a general discussion about Steve's fear of an Albanian threat and Fearnley went on to say that Steve had often spoken about Ben as something of a mentor. Consequently, they'd decided as a team and in consultation with the paper's editor that they'd like Ben to write the Herald's obituary of Steve. As it was a Friday, the last obit that Steve had written, about a belly dancer from Batley who had managed to come second in Turkmenistan's Got Talent, had been published. The next Friday slot would be reserved for Steve's obituary, in memory of their most popular obit writer. At first, Ben was reluctant, arguing that he really wasn't in the right frame of mind at present and that he may lack objectivity.

"I understand completely," said Fearnley. "This isn't laziness on our part, Ben, we firmly believe that you are the best person to write this since you were not only a friend but you are also an obituary writer from an organisation that prides itself on impartiality and besides, you have several days in which to prepare it." Eventually, though reluctantly, Ben agreed on condition that the BBC was happy about the idea. Fearnley said he would take care of that matter and would get hold of the Herald's personnel file on Steve to help with biographical details. Finally, Fearnley mentioned that a writer named Patrick Quartermain had been trying to contact Steve several times in the past fortnight but Steve had failed to return any of his calls. Today, on hearing the news about Steve's murder, Quartermain had contacted Fearnley asking that whoever would write Steve's obituary should contact him first since he possessed certain information that would be highly pertinent to it. Fearnley passed the contact details to Ben who agreed to ring him. When Ben put down the phone, he had a feeling that he'd let himself in for more than he'd bargained.

23 SUSPECTS

DCI Susan Medlock looked exhausted as she walked slowly into the incident room where the dozen or so members of her team had gathered. For the past two days she had spent hours grilling members of the Albanian gang responsible for such a catalogue of misery for hundreds of women captured abroad and forced into a corrupting life of sleaze. Strewn around the room were newspapers with headlines screaming about the involvement of Carla Wilson's fiancé in her murder. All of the publications referred to Carla Wilson's presentation of an edition of Crimecrunchers that had focused on the outrageous paucity of action by the various authorities on curbing this modern-day slave trade. Like the obituarist who has to write a piece on someone they knew personally and admired, so Steve's death had been one out of the ordinary in the many deaths with which she had to deal on a regular basis. It was a genuine shock to her hard-nosed character that someone who only hours earlier had been helping her with her inquiries in both a positive and entertaining way, and one who had feared for his own safety for which she had been largely unable to help, had been murdered. What's more, she had had to front more than one media conference with both the UK and foreign press baying for more information than she was able to give. Then, as she was successfully navigating her course through a perplexing case in which the involvement of Gordon Gunter and his henchmen added a further complication, came the murder of Steve Graham. The ghost of Irina was once again evoked, and there were far too many so far unanswerable questions raised. At least now she was facing her own colleagues.

"I'd just like to say a big thank you and congratulations to all of you who have helped not only yesterday but throughout the course of this investigation. We finally got the result we were looking for and I'm as confident as I can be that we've netted the big fish of this Albanian gang and that they'll go down for a long time. So a big thanks to all of you. You will be aware that the suspect known as Costas Archimedes, the fiancé of Ms Wilson is the only exception. As some of you may be aware, he turns out not to be who he says he is. In reality, he appears to be an Albanian national called Murat Bardulla operating on a false Greek passport. He has disappeared, most probably abroad, and Interpol are on the case. We have gathered plenty of evidence to suggest he was part of the gang and we suspect he was involved in the murders of both his fiancée and of Irina Lockyer. I'm confident that he will be found and arrested soon."

A smattering of applause broke out and more thanks were exchanged among the assembled. Medlock then asked DI Beavon to recount the events of the previous day in more detail. Five minutes later when he had finished his report and questions were answered, DCI Medlock took the floor again.

"The other reason I've called this meeting concerns this fellow here." She turned to a picture of Steve Graham pinned on an adjoining board.

"As you will be aware, Stephen Graham was murdered on a train yesterday. Some of you will also be aware that there may or may not be a connection with the case we've just hopefully solved. One door closes and another one opens, in this case a train carriage door. He was an important potential witness in the gang members' forthcoming trial since he gave us the lead on a car the gang used a couple of days before the killing of Irina Lockyer. He was worried that he might have become a target as a potential prosecution witness and his murder puts members of this gang in the frame. Over the course of our further interrogation of the Albanians we shall be seeking to discover whether or not this holds up. The description we have been given of the suspected killer is threadbare to say the least. He was wearing a mask, dark glasses and a hoodie and appears to have been hiding in the toilet before pouncing on his prey."

"Are we certain it was a man, Guv?" asked one of the female detective constables.

"The CCTV pictures showing the suspect running away suggest a man. The pictures don't reveal exactly how he or she left the station since the camera trained on the ticket barriers was not working. CCTV cameras outside the station show crowds of people. The suspect may have been among them; the pictures are inconclusive. We are appealing for witnesses. No one has yet come forward but it's early days. The murder weapon was the usual sharp bladed instrument, as yet to be found. The blade pierced the unfortunate victim's heart. Was this a lucky shot from the attacker or the work of a professional, and was he or she operating on his own or in cahoots with others? These are among the questions we will address."

There were nods from some of those listening.

"There is a possibility that the attacker may have escaped over a set of railings on the station platform. Officers and the forensic team are searching for clues as we speak. The day before, Mr Graham had a run-in with a man on the train, one Zachariah Clarides, a British man of Greek Cypriot heritage. Many people witnessed it and this Mr Clarides appears to have come off worse. He has a motive therefore but we're still trying to locate him. However, we will find him. Some of you may have also seen in the file a note from DI Beavon that Mr Graham had reported to us that he was being followed by a man, with what he called a swarthy complexion, with a distinctive mark on his face – a 'hairy wart' was his description. However, after speaking to his widow yesterday, it appears that this man was in the employ of her father who was under the impression that he was having a bit on the side and had decided to have him followed, so we have eliminated him from our enquiries. Anyway, there was no mention of a wart, hairy or otherwise, in any of the descriptions of the suspect."

This provoked one or two chuckles from the floor.

"Finally, Mr Graham who was a journalist on The National Herald, had written an obituary on Gordon Gunter, the bloke who inflicted the pink stretch limo on to all of our lives. He had a bit of form."

"Yes, he got 20 years for bad taste, Guv." More laughs.

"Thank you, Barry, your contribution is always welcome. He was done for cottaging in the 1960s and this was mentioned in the obituary, as was the fact that he had a particular liking for underage boys. That is something else we will have to look into. Apparently, he told a friend that Mr Gunter's brother Fred who objected to the mention of this had threatened him in a phone call. So he will need checking out."

"We'll bend over backwards on that one, Guv."

"Thank you Barry, I knew I could trust you to be meticulous in your political correctness. I will be convening another meeting tomorrow and I will assign duties then. We're in the very early stages of this investigation and we all have to familiarise ourselves more with the case but for now I have some Albanians to interrogate. Are there any questions?"

"Yes, Guv," answered Barry. "Did this geezer with the wart find any evidence of this Graham bloke playing away?"

"Not as far as we know but we've only spoken to the widow so far, not him, but yes that's a good point. I assume you're thinking of a jealous husband?"

"That sort of thing, yeah."

"Well you've just assigned yourself a job, Barry. Any more questions?"

"Yes, guv, what does this Fred Gunter do for a job?"

"I'm led to believe he's a scrap metal dealer, Barry." More laughter.

"Open and shut case then, Guv."

"If only we could rely on stereotypes, Barry. Any more questions?"

"Yes, just one, Guv. Is there any relevance to this bloke who he hit on the train being a Greek Cypriot?"

“I said he was of Greek Cypriot heritage, Barry. As for the relevance, I don’t think the argument concerned the rights and wrongs of the UN mandate over Cyprus. They were arguing over a seat I believe.” There was more laughter.

“Any more questions? No? We’ll reconvene at 1000 hours here tomorrow. Thank you.”

24 PATRICK

When suicide bombers struck the tube and bus service in London in 2005 killing 52 people and injuring hundreds more, a local TV crew interviewed Ben and others about how they felt commuting into the city the next day. Ben told the reporter that his coming to work was an act of defiance, that not to do so would be giving into terrorism and that it was a statement of not surrendering to evil. Though he may have felt those sentiments, the truth was that like everyone else he had to pay the mortgage and there was no other convenient way of getting to work anyhow. In other words, you just had to get on with life. Those thoughts ran through his mind as he rode to the station that morning. The thought of taking the train on which he'd seen his friend murdered such a short time ago made him nervous but there was little alternative. As Elizabeth had said, it was akin to driving a car again quickly after an accident before it became a psychological problem. When he arrived on the platform an anonymous person had placed a bunch of flowers under the information monitor with a note that simply read "Steve RIP".

Ben had not intended travelling today since he was still in shock. The events of the tragedy continued to play in his mind. However, once the BBC had agreed that he should write Steve's obit he had something with which to occupy himself and in that regard he'd taken a call from the writer Patrick Quartermain and had arranged to meet him at his central London hotel. Though he'd not heard of Quartermain, a quick google had established that he was a successful and acclaimed writer of popular history books and he was intrigued as to what possible information he might possess that would have any bearing on Steve's obituary. A brief phone call had not yielded anything since Quartermain said that it was a somewhat complicated story that would better be recounted over a drink or a cup of coffee. A testament to Quartermain's success as a writer was reflected in the swankiness of his hotel. Ben was ushered into the reception area by a flunky and every manner of designer label was on display among the guests milling about. When

Quartermain appeared within minutes of his being informed of Ben's arrival, he was adorned in an expensive-looking light cream suit with a scarlet silk lining, and matching carnation in his buttonhole. Ben was tempted to ask him where the wedding was.

"Mr Murray, delighted to meet you old chap."

"Please, call me Ben."

"And you must call me Patrick. Right Ben, what will you have? Too early for a little snifter?"

"Coffee's fine for me. But don't let me..."

"Coffee will do me fine, dear boy."

Coffee was ordered and came served in beautiful porcelain cups and saucers. The small talk that followed consisted of questions about their different "lines of country" within their respective creative fields and a brief discussion about the merits of television history series. Then it was down to business. Patrick took out a sheaf of photocopied documents typed in German. He explained that he had spent the last year researching a book on the attempts by the former East German State Security Service, the STASI, to spread its insidious tentacles to Britain by spying on certain individuals. It was part of a pattern of espionage that was conducted by Communist states during the Cold War that ended after the collapse of the Berlin wall in 1989. It was while he was working in the Stasi archive in Berlin earlier in the year that he'd happened upon a file concerning an Englishman with the codename "Schnitz". The file, from which the photocopies on the table were taken, told in fine detail how Schnitz had been seconded to Berlin's Dynamo Sports Academy, as part of his course in sports psychology at Leeds University. East Germany had poured large amounts of money into sport as a form of propaganda. While there, Schnitz had fallen in love with a pole vaulter by the name of Britta Schopenhauer. The file included addresses, telephone numbers, reports of where they socialised, names of friends, the registration number of their Trabant and even what time of day each left their apartment. The detail, explained Patrick, illustrated the extent of the Stasi's reach and the paranoia that underpinned its existence.

"Reading it made me feel like a voyeur, the amount of trivial detail beggared belief," the author admitted before sipping from his coffee cup.

Quartermain speculated that the couple were much in love because an application was made for Britta to obtain an exit visa in order to visit Schnitz when his secondment ended. There then followed much discussion between members of the Stasi and its foreign intelligence arm, the HVA, over whether this should be granted. Normally there would have been little chance, but some official in the HVA suggested that Schnitz might serve a useful purpose. It transpired from the file that Schnitz's secondment had been approved unofficially because he had taken part in a CND march in Leeds and was a member of the Socialist Society at the university. It devised a plan in which it would offer Britta an exit visa on condition that Schnitz supplied information on certain academics and fellow students.

"Basically," explained Quatermain, "the regime wanted this Schnitz fellow to be one of their 'spotters', keeping tabs on certain people abroad with the aim possibly of recruiting them."

Quatermain went on to relate that after Schnitz returned to England he did send certain low-grade information about a certain head of the politics department but the file concludes rather abruptly by suggesting that the scheme was not likely to bear much fruit and should be terminated. No mention was made of any granting of the exit visa. At this point, Ben, who had been listening intently, interjected.

"I think I see where you're going with this. You're going to tell me that Schnitz was Steve Graham."

"Exactly, I've checked the university secondees list for that year and he's the only one that fits the bill in terms of time and place though his actual name is never mentioned. Were you aware of these things?"

"No, not at all. I only recently learned that he had been in East Berlin but he never mentioned this Schopenschnitzel."

"Schopenhauer."

"The thing is that I didn't know Steve all that well. Yes, I knew him for a long time and we enjoyed each other's company on the train and shared a profession and so on but we didn't socialise much bar the odd drink before catching the train or at Christmas. We were commuter friends basically. What's more I'm 10 or so years older than him. I have to say too that he wasn't very forthcoming about revealing too much about himself; perfect spy material by the sound of it yet I can't believe he would betray his country."

"Ah, but it's blackmail, dear chap. These devils in the Stasi were masters at it. There's nothing like the love of a good woman to use as a tool for manipulating a man's mind."

Ben nodded in agreement and sipped his coffee. "I gather you spoke to Steve. What did he say?"

"Absolutely nothing, hung up on me each time I rang."

"Well that speaks volumes I guess. What about Schnopenschnitz?"

"Schopenhauer."

"What about her? Have you talked to her?"

Quartermain began sifting through a pile of papers. "Well I've spent a lot of time and energy trying to track her down and I've discovered that she is married under another name and that she still lives in Berlin but is currently in Britain on a three-month course studying English."

"How did you discover that?"

"I spoke to her husband on the phone when I finally found out where she lived. I was posing as an old friend but when I asked her where she was staying he clammed up and wouldn't say. I guess living with the Stasi has made all East Germans a bit wary, old bean."

Ben was tempted to ask him at what time she left the house each day but decided that the irony might not be appreciated.

"And this academic, does he know about this?"

"I believe so. He's an Emeritus Professor at Leeds named Colin Tether. I tried phoning him and left messages but he didn't return my calls. So I wrote to him explaining my findings."

Ben looked into the distance as he computed in his mind these new facts about his dead friend.

"I expect this professor wouldn't have been exactly overjoyed at the news."

"Too right, old thing."

"What about Maria, Steve's wife? She might know something."

"Well I didn't want to speak to her without speaking first to him and now that he's just been killed I think it's not really very good timing wouldn't you say, old chap?"

Ben nodded. "No, of course not. Look, I'm going to have to talk to her myself pretty soon because the Herald have asked me to write his obituary. I may well have to raise this matter since from what you're saying to me I presume you're going to publish this anyway, you're just looking for confirmation."

"On the button, old boy."

"Well leave it with me Patrick and I'll get back to you."

"Here's my card."

"Thank you and thanks for the coffee."

"Well thank you dear chap and my heartiest condolences on the loss of your friend."

With that, and with a million thoughts stirring in an already over-stimulated brain, Ben took a last gulp of coffee, rose and bade Patrick goodbye. He headed for his office. Although his boss had granted him as much leave as he'd like to help him recover from the trauma, something Patrick had said had reminded him that after Steve had fought with Albie he'd handed him an envelope in the pub for safekeeping. He'd locked it in his desk drawer.

The surprise, when Ben walked through his office door, was palpable. The Stick immediately walked up to him and put both her skinny arms around his waist. Both Anthony and Keith wore expressions of serious concern that he'd never witnessed before, not even when Michael Jackson died without an up-to-date obit ready to broadcast. These remained while Ben sat down and recounted the events on the train. At one point tears welled up in his eyes and Anthony had to provide him with a cup of water from the cooler. Anthony was convinced that the killer was connected to the Gunters. "Anyone associated with that bunch of crooks could be guilty of anything including murder." Gradually, their expressions morphed from sympathetic to mischievous inquisitiveness when Ben raised the subject of the envelope that Steve had handed to him for safekeeping. Ben had mislaid the key somewhere in the office, which gave them time to speculate as to its contents in a manner that broke the overwrought atmosphere. Suggestions included a key to a safe deposit box that contained The Holy Grail, a secret will that left all of Steve's money to a camel sanctuary in Timbuktu, and a birth certificate that proved that Steve was in fact the love child of Anne Widdecombe. Having learnt of the Berlin connection, Anthony began imitating Marlene Dietrich singing Falling in Love Again. The Stick, impatient with both the flippancy of her office mates and with Ben's delay in locating the drawer key, believed they had to be the love-letters from a mistress. So, when the key was found and Ben removed the envelope from it, there developed an air of eager anticipation. The result was initially baffling and anticlimactic. The contents comprised a set of family photographs of a couple and child clearly taken over several years. There were no letters included or obvious clues as to the people's identity. The atmosphere in the room deflated like a balloon that had been stuck with a pin. Anthony began singing a Who song, Can't Explain, still in a Marlene Dietrich voice. Keith suggested a game of computer golf to improve the mood. The Stick suggested Ben should take a holiday to recharge his batteries.

"You should take a holiday on a fat farm," said Anthony to The Stick.

"You should know, you must have been on hundreds," was the Stick's immediate riposte.

"Anyway, I can't afford a holiday," she continued, "on a fat farm or anywhere else."

"I thought you were rich. Didn't your boyfriend steal your yacht?" asked Anthony.

"He stole my boat. I live on a little island on the Thames. It's quicker to row the few yards across than walk up to the bridge, or at least it was until he took the boat."

"Why did he steal it?"

"If you really want to know it's because I wouldn't share a threesome with him and his friend Gilbert."

Anthony shook his head. "Too much information."

While his colleagues were trading insults and banter, Ben had noticed a compliments slip that he had somehow missed inside the outer envelope. Printed on it was the address of the Victoria Hotel, London SW1 together with the telephone number. When he showed it to the room, the excitement returned. Ben picked up the phone, pressed the numbers and waited for the answer.

"Hello, Victoria Hotel."

"May I speak to Britta Schnippenhofer please."

"Britta Schopenhauer. Just a minute."

Ben could feel the sweat oozing into the palms of his hands.

"Hallo. Britta."

"Hello Britta. My name's Ben Murray, I'm a friend of Steve Graham."

There was a pause.

"How did you get my number?"

Ben was not sure how to answer her. "He gave me something that I think belonged to you. I need to speak to you please, Britta."

Ben had to wait a few seconds for a response.

"Can you come to my hotel?"

Ben's heart leapt. He looked at his colleagues with a look that said "bull's-eye".

"Yes, I'm half an hour away."

"Give me an hour please."

"Of course, see you in an hour."

As he rang off he looked towards his colleagues' bemused faces.

"I'll explain all later."

At that, Anthony, still in Dietrich mode, started singing the Hokey Kokey.

"Een aht, een aht, shake it all abaaaaht."

25 BRITTA

It was raining steadily by the time Ben emerged from Victoria underground station. The first inkling of winter was announcing itself through the iciness that he felt on his fingers and the tip of his nose. He glanced up at a street sign to set his bearings and, placing a newspaper over his head to shield the worst of the rain, marched towards the Victoria Hotel. When he arrived a few minutes later the place turned out to be much as expected, a collection of four bed-sits manned by a receptionist who sat opposite a bucket catching raindrops gently falling through a crack in the ceiling. It was the first sight to greet Ben as he entered, and the lady shrugged her shoulders in a wordless apology. He asked for Britta without attempting the surname and the receptionist rang her to announce Ben's arrival. When she appeared at her door Ben's first impression was how tall she was, an aspect that hadn't been so obvious from the photographs. Then he remembered that she had been a pole-vaulter where height was presumably an essential attribute to success. She was slim, blue-eyed and blonde and immediately he could see why Steve had fallen for her. However, Britta looked as tired and dejected as one would expect from one who had just lost a friend in the most sudden and horrific manner. The pair shook hands, looked sympathetically at each other and then hugged one another. It seemed entirely natural under the circumstances even though this was the first time they'd met.

"Whoever could have done this awful thing?" were Britta's first words spoken in almost flawless English. Ben felt that it was too early to use this as a cue for a bout of speculation, and just nodded his head.

"I have this feeling that it is my fault. I meet Steve again after so many years and suddenly he is dead."

"I'm sure it's just a tragic coincidence," said Ben placing a reassuring hand on her shoulder. Britta dried her tears with a tissue and offered Ben coffee, which he was glad to accept. She explained that she had come to London for a three-month advanced English language course, which the import-export company for which she worked was funding. She was already in her final month but after Steve's murder she just wanted to go home. She wondered about staying for the funeral but she had no idea when it might be and guessed that it would take more time than usual to be arranged given the circumstances. After Ben described watching his friend die in front of him, they exchanged teary smiles in a kind of sympathetic solidarity. Britta then decided that something stronger was called for and produced a bottle of Schnapps and Ben, blowing his nose and wiping his eyes, replied to her invitation to join her in a drop with just a nod and a smile. She also came up with two liqueur glasses, unusual items for a cheap hotel to stock, thought Ben. He wondered if they were part of Britta's normal travel accoutrements along with flight pillow and travel wash. The ensuing relaxation courtesy of the alcohol instigated an outpouring of shared memories of their mutual friend. Britta explained how she had been instantly attracted to Steve who would watch her train and would joke with her much to the annoyance of her coach. With such an imposing and tough training schedule, Steve was such a blessed relief and so much fun. What's more, she helped him with his German and he with her English.

"He was so unlike any of the other boys I'd known, so passionate, so many opinions about everything."

"Opinionated he certainly was," replied Ben inwardly marvelling at her English and many other things about her.

"My coach didn't like me to go out during the week even though I was 20 years old. He was such a man for discipline, you know. But Steve discovered a way I could sneak past the man at the front gate, and we would go dancing or drinking with friends. We were young and it was so exciting. I loved, how you say, the thrill."

Ben smiled as he caught her enthusiasm as she stared into the distance as her memories came flooding back.

"Yes, I remember Steve telling me about the building that replaced the Berlin Palace where he used to go," said Ben.

"Ah yes. 'Erich's Lamp Shop', we called it, you know after Erich Honecker, our glorious leader," she replied with a feigned scowl. "We would often go bowling there."

"That's the one they demolished after the wall came down."

"Ja, that's the one."

Britta described further the lifestyle she enjoyed with Steve that proved such a contrast to the intense atmosphere of the sports academy. He introduced her to so many aspects of life outside of sport of which she had had little experience. She and other East Germans were fed endless propaganda about a system that was gradually failing. Steve would compare it to one of Berlin's cabarets where a man is pretending everything is normal as his trousers start to fall around his ankles. Ben concurred on how passionate Steve could be, obsessive almost. He then apologised to Britta for having to bring up the matter that Patrick Quartermain had raised regarding the Stasi and the promised exit visa. That provoked a change in Britta's demeanour and tone.

"This was a very difficult period for me, Ben. The Stasi watched everybody. They didn't like their people being with a foreigner, a foreigner from the West anyway. I didn't care about those pigs but they could take away my scholarship so we had to be careful. I was young and fearless in those days and it was so wonderful to be having fun."

"Yes, I remember those days...just," said Ben. Britta gave a flirtatious smile but continued in serious vein.

"You see, Steve was very much in love with me but it started to get how you say, very serious and that frightened me. He talked of marriage and going back to England. I liked him of course but the idea of marrying someone at my age and when I was in the middle of my training, well it took me by surprise."

Her remark took Ben by surprise and he gave an understanding nod.

"When he said to me, Britta, come back with me I told him there was no chance of the people here allowing me to do that. But, you know, Steve never is taking no for an answer. He kept telling to me, would you come with me if they are giving me an exit visa? I said to him I would because I knew that they would not allow it. I should have been honest with him and told him that he was rushing me."

Ben looked quizzically at Britta. "Would you have married him if he had decided to live with you in East Berlin?"

"I don't think so, no, but that would never have happened anyway. I think you say in English a hypothetical situation."

"Spoken like a native, Britta."

"Thank you. You know, if he hadn't been so intense with me, maybe things might have been different."

Ben sipped his schnapps and felt his eyes water and his throat burn. This was a potent brew.

"So when he applied for an exit visa, you weren't really serious about leaving Berlin?"

"No. My family lived here and my friends. And then there was my training. It was all too much, and then there was something else."

"Before you tell me what that was, did you ever discover why Mr Quartermain wanted to speak to you?"

Britta looked puzzled. "You mean that English writer?"

Ben nodded.

"My husband spoke to him on the telephone and said he was writing a book about the Stasi and then a couple of weeks ago I contacted Steve here. I knew where he worked and we met again for the first time in 20 years or more. I was very nervous, you know, about seeing him again but he was just the way he was when we first met, so charming, so funny. Steve told me that this Quartermain had been trying to contact him. He hadn't spoken to him but he guessed what it was about. When he told me what he'd done I was, how do you say, dumbfund..."

"Dumbfounded."

"Ja, dumbfounded. It was like in our Goethe play, Faust, do you know?"

"Yes, he made a Faustian pact, a pact with the Devil."

"Ja, exactly. I couldn't believe it. I couldn't believe that first he would do such a thing for the Stasi, and I couldn't believe that he thought they would give me a visa. Those people were bastards, you know."

"So you believe the Stasi would have double-crossed him."

"Double-cross?"

"I mean, they would have never have kept their word."

"No, never, never, never. Besides, at that time, I was a star of the GDR athletics team. I went abroad many times to compete but we were guarded like prisoners and they would never have let me leave for good."

Britta reached for the Schnapps and refilled both glasses without asking Ben. She then began speaking about life in East Germany and told quite heart-breaking stories of how people she knew had tried in vain to escape over the wall, two of them dying on the barbed wire. She wasn't brave enough to try especially as she and her family led a relatively cosseted life thanks to her athletic prowess. Before long, she reached for the bottle again and despite Ben's feeble protests, poured them both another shot. Ben could feel his head becoming lighter and fire in his cheeks. He knew that he always became very touchy feely when drunk. He reckoned that at the rate they were drinking he'd soon be suggesting that he and she should run away and commit bigamy together. Britta hadn't talked about the past for so long and it was clearly having an unsettling effect. Ben then asked her why she had decided to re-establish contact with Steve after such a long time. She paused, took a deep breath and exhaled strongly. She looked Ben in the face as she began what was to be her confession.

"That's what I was telling you before. Just after Steve left Berlin to go back to England I discovered I was pregnant." She paused for a reaction but Ben was so surprised he could think of nothing to say. Finally he said something, the wrong thing.

"Was it definitely his?"

"Ben, who do you take me for?" she said with mock outrage.

"I'm sorry, Britta, I didn't mean to imply anything, I...."

Britta smiled and continued. "It was an even bigger shock for me than the shock I see on your face right now."

Ben gulped his Schnapps. Suddenly he remembered the family photographs Steve had given him.

"And you had the child?"

"Ja ja, I had the child. I thought about an abortion and my coach was furious with me and begged me to have one and I nearly agreed to do so but in the end I could not go through with it and when my parents offered to help me bring the baby up I decided to have the baby. He was born on 2nd February 1989."

"What was Steve's reaction when you told him?"

"I didn't tell him. Not until this week."

Ben was shocked at this revelation. Things were beginning to fall into place. Steve must have heard this bombshell, that he'd fathered a child with Britta, just before Hilary found him sitting on the tube station floor.

Doubtless he'd had a few glasses of Schnapps too. It occurred to him that Britta might have been the cause for Steve going missing that led to the telephone call from Maria.

"He had no idea you'd given birth to his child?"

"I could not tell him. If he knew he would push to come back or try to make me come to him. He was a good man. He was not the type to abandon a child. But I had already decided that although I loved being with Steve, I only ever thought of our relationship as like a holiday romance. I never wanted marriage not even when I discovered I was going to have a child. I felt that I was too young to commit myself to someone I was not completely sure about."

She paused and looked out at the rain that was beating hard against the window.

"So what made you decide to tell him this week?"

Britta took a sip of Schnapps and related the story. She explained first that her child was named Klaus and was now 23 years old and training to be a doctor. She had met her husband Werner not long after Klaus's birth and married him within a year. He raised Klaus as if he were his own and since the child knew no other "parent" than Werner, the couple felt that it would be better for the child to grow up in ignorant bliss of his real biological heritage especially since Britta had heard nothing further from Steve after their relationship ended finally. In fact, Britta had almost forgotten that Steve was the father until one day last year Klaus discovered Werner's blood group. He realised that he couldn't be related and confronted his mother.

"I had to tell him everything and it was a great trauma for him. He kept asking why, why, why we didn't tell him. I said to him we did it for him, only for him."

She explained that it took Klaus several weeks to come to terms with his discovery but he settled down. His relations with Werner had always been good and the couple thought that the matter was closed. However, a few weeks ago, Klaus raised the question again by suggesting he would like to meet his real father. He had googled him and learned so much about Steve and his work. Despite Britta's attempts to dissuade him, he was adamant, so the family decided that when Britta came to England for her language course, she would contact Steve and explain everything to him.

"What was Steve's reaction when you first spoke to him?"

"Well when we met here again, we had a wonderful time, so wonderful that I decided not to tell him about Klaus straight away. The third time we met though I told him. He was astonished again and very angry with me. He was like his son, always asking me why, why, why I did not tell him. Then I showed him some photos, you know, of Klaus with Werner and me. He looked at them for such a long time. I could see tears in his eyes and he asked me if he could keep them and I say sure they're for you."

Ben reached into his breast pocket for the photographs that Steve had given him.

"I have them here."

Britta was taken by surprise.

"The day before Steve died he handed me an envelope asking me to keep them for him in case anything happened to him. I opened it later and found these. That's how I knew how to find you because it had the hotel notepaper inside it."

"But why did he give them to you?"

"I expect he didn't want his wife to find them and ask who these people were. I think his marriage was going through a difficult period and maybe the knowledge that he had a son by someone else might have complicated things further."

“I see,” said Britta looking pensive.

“You might as well keep these now, Britta,” said Ben handing over the envelope. “Your son will never see his father after all.”

The revelations had a sobering effect on Ben. They chatted for another half hour about Steve’s nature, Ben having explained that he had to write the obituary. As he was thinking about leaving, Britta’s phone rang. It was the receptionist explaining that a policeman had arrived to see her. Ben saw the worried look on her face and explained that it was probably because a man following Steve had given them her address. He was referring to the Hairy Wart. Looking decidedly confused, she went out to meet the policeman who flashed his ID and introduced himself as Detective Inspector Barry Perkins. Ben then introduced himself as the friend of Steve’s who had witnessed his death. DI Perkins explained that his enquiries were entirely of a routine nature and would take little time. Ben saw this as his cue to leave. He and Britta hugged each other again and promised to keep in touch. As Ben made his way back to the tube, he couldn’t help but wonder how Steve, who always insisted on revealing everything in his obituaries, would have written his own were it possible.

26 FINALE

Someone once wrote of Sir Thomas Lawrence, Marquis of Hertford, 1769 – 1830, "No man ever lived more despised or died less regretted." Ben had never heard such excoriation, however elegant, from acquaintances of the bereaved that he'd encountered. He found that dealing with widows, widowers or the partners of the departed was quite often the most pleasing aspect of preparing an obituary. It seemed to Ben that they often found it a release; a kind of therapy to answer questions about their loved ones' lives. He had come across spouses embittered by the actions of others who had tried to thwart the career ambitions of their partners, tempted him or her to infidelity or treated them unjustly in some way. However, in general, death would in the majority of cases produce a feeling of serenity in the grieving who would be flattered and content to co-operate with the writing of a prestigious public farewell that an obituary would engender.

However, when your husband dies suddenly and violently all bets are off. When Maria's father passed the phone to his daughter when he rang her the following morning needing to glean details for his obit, she was inconsolable. She was angry with Steve for having been killed and leaving her alone with her two young children. She was angry with him for the way he seemed to have invited trouble for himself in all shapes and varieties. She was angry with him for being so uncompromising in his beliefs and attitudes. Above all, she felt guilty at not being the wife she felt he required. All of this came pouring out over the telephone for almost an hour with Ben able only to interject with the occasional platitude. Understandably, Maria was an emotional churn still trying to come to terms with an horrific event that would affect her life and that of her family forever. It made it rather difficult for Ben to ask such mundane questions as where Steve was born and what school he attended. In the end, Maria felt even guiltier for speaking so long without asking Ben how he felt having watched Steve die. She promised that she would try to answer biographical details as best and as soon as she was able by email. In the meantime, she gave Ben the names of two of Steve's closest friends. Ben typed the list of questions and emailed them soon after he put down the phone. He included one that read, "What do you know of Steve's stay in East Berlin during the late 1980s?"

The contacts that Maria gave him proved very useful in providing him with a flavour of Steve as a journalist and as a friend. One contact led to another. A good newspaper obituary he felt should contain short anecdotes that shed light on a person's character. Most anecdotes were too long, some unprintable, but a short, pithy and relevant one was gold dust. Ben called seven or eight of Steve's friends or colleagues. The journalists among them were more eloquent in their descriptions and far less prone to using clichés. He was writing up his notes after one telephone interview when his mobile sounded. It was Patrick Quartermain. The call brought good news. He had at last managed to contact Professor Tether, the academic whom Steve had allegedly reported on for the Stasi. Patrick passed on his number and told Ben that he was expecting a call. When Ben duly rang him the professor was still dazed and the pair talked for almost 20 minutes. When Maria's email arrived later that day, it mentioned only that Steve had had a girlfriend in East Berlin but nothing more on that score.

Earlier that morning, DCI Medlock had visited the train station where Steve's killer had got away. She looked closely at the fence over which the culprit had escaped and she ruminated over who might have been responsible as she walked slowly up and down the platform. This looked like a well-planned operation possibly involving more than one person. Beyond the fence, down a grassy bank, was a road on which a getaway car could have laid in wait though nobody had witnessed one. Certainly whoever scaled the fence, given its size, would have had to be agile. Around her were two forensic investigators carrying out a fingertip search. As she wandered along the platform trying to piece together what few clues she had, her phone had rung. In a voice laden with excitement DI Beavon announced that a body had been discovered floating in the Thames near Rotherhithe. It was Carla Wilson's fiancé.

DCI Medlock broke the news to a hastily convened media conference. She was forced to bat away questions she was either not prepared or was unable to divulge. She was, however, able to inform of the arrest of several members of the Albanian gang over the Irina murder. She had carefully stuck to the facts of the case and later found it necessary to stonewall accusations that the police were not taking the issue of people trafficking seriously enough. She was tempted to say, "Give us the funds and we'll do a proper job," but she was experienced enough to know when to say nothing. The crime correspondent of The Herald then asked her if she believed there was a link between the Albanian gang and the death of their obituary writer. She was subjected to much speculation and tittle-tattle and she branded it as such. She was able to be more specific when addressing her team at their later than usual morning meeting.

"Right, listen up everyone." She waited as the general murmur of conversation died down. "We have a significant development in the Stephen Graham case." She paused again as a ripple of excitement at her announcement rose and fell. "Forensics have discovered a pair of dark glasses near a fence by the side of the platform at the station from where the assailant fled. They were laying in some undergrowth the other side of the fence near the road. Dark glasses are not commonly worn by people in November especially when the sun doesn't shine, in other words most days, so it's looking hopeful. They're also of the wrap-around variety described by several witnesses on the train. I'm told they have a print and we're waiting to see if we have a match. We would have had it checked earlier but for a computer problem." There was a collective groan.

"However, I'm told the system's up and running again. I'll let you know in due course. Meanwhile, Annie did you check on Mr Clarides, the man who he was fighting on the train?"

Annie, not expecting to be asked so quickly, stiffened. "Yes, Guv. He seemed as shocked as anyone. He had reported the victim for assault and I don't see that investigating him further is likely to yield anything."

"Right, thanks Annie. Barry, how did you get on with the Victoria lead?"

"Another dead end I think, Guv. It turned out to be an old friend from Germany over here on a language course, nothing more. She had an alibi. And I met Ben Murray there, Mr Graham's friend and it seems there was nothing suspicious. She was a former pole-vaulter and I can tell you, she could vault my pole anytime." Another collective groan rang out.

"Barry, she wouldn't have to jump very high to vault your pole I'm sure." The answer provoked laughter and jeers.

"That's not what you told me last night, Guv." There were "ooohs" from colleagues at his brazen cheek.

"In your dreams, Perkins," said Medlock forcing a pained smile.

"Now, Geoff how did you get on with our friend the scrap metal dealer?"

Before Geoff could answer, DI Beavon walked into the room clutching a piece of paper and wearing a broad smile.

"Dum da da dum, we have a match," he announced proudly, waving the paper in the air before handing it to his boss. DCI Medlock looked carefully at the content for a few seconds, took a deep breath and addressed her colleagues.

"Aga Demir, a vicious little bastard with two convictions for GBH. Bit of a psycho by the look of this. Lives in Enfield. Demir, Demir, where have I heard that name?"

"It's a Blondie song, Guv," answered Barry.

"It's not a Blondie song, shut it Barry."

"Guv", cried Barry excitedly. "Demir was the name of the bloke who Gordon Gunter was doing the business with on Hampstead Heath who our man mentioned in the obituary."

Medlock paused and as Barry's observation hit home, her face suddenly beamed. "That's it, that's our connection. Barry, your pole rating has just gone up."

There were cheers, as Barry looked decidedly pleased with himself.

" I'm closing this meeting. Everyone, get tooled up, I'll inform the heavy boys and we'll pay this man a visit."

As he sat at his computer preparing to write Steve's obituary, Ben was working out in his mind the tone he would adopt. Writing about a friend required an injection of personal warmth and detail, while maintaining objectivity. Since he didn't socialise often with Steve, this seemed to him easier than it might have been had they been closer. More difficult though were two questions he needed to consider. Should he inform on Steve's treachery, despite its being short-lived and low-grade, and should he mention the child Steve never knew he had fathered until shortly before his death? Steve's words about the dead deserving the truth echoed through his mind. However, Ben couldn't rid himself of the notion that had Steve been able to write his own obituary he might well have left out certain information that he would have been only too pleased to include in someone else's. If he had been secretive about the Stasi blackmail during his lifetime, would he be so intent on having his reputation stained by the revelation in his obituary? What would his young children feel once they had grown up to understand the implications? On the other hand, it was done out of love rather than personal profit. And there was Prof. Colin Tether to consider too. Wouldn't he resent its omission? If he did, he would need to inform Maria before publication. She would not be happy. Hilary, with whom he had discussed the issue, had been undecided on this question but she was adamant that no mention should be made of the child. "Let sleeping dogs lie," she had said. Would it be better though to wake the dog now than have it bite hard in future years? Ben could hear Steve arguing that obituaries were written for the newspaper's readers, not the family. The words "truth, truth, truth" rang in his brain. In the end, he made a judgement based not on the whole truth but on what he thought was appropriate.

On Friday morning, the following obituary appeared in The National Herald.

STEPHEN ANTHONY GRAHAM

Journalist.

By Ben Murray

In this space over the past two and a half years, Steve Graham built up a reputation as a champion of the common man and woman in his obituary column. Whether it was the stalwart of the parent teacher's association, the 80-year-old cross-Channel swimmer, the incontinent zoo-keeper or the Salvation Army tuba player, Steve gave national recognition in death to those whose achievements went unnoticed outside their social environ. His column achieved such status that he was inundated with suggestions for subjects. His criteria for those he chose included personal achievements, quirkiness and amusement. The tale of the Morris dancer with the frog down his trousers performing for The Queen continues to make me smile.

Steve's choice of obit subjects should be seen in the broader context of his belief that the achievements of so-called ordinary people did not always receive due recognition in society as a whole. Steve believed that successive governments, obsessed with the high financiers and so-called wealth creators, had derided the status of public sector workers such as teachers, nurses, social workers and the like. Bankers and successful businessmen he left to his colleagues' obituary columns. Steve despised the "fame for fame's sake" culture that had grown in recent times. He did not eschew celebrity per se; but celebrities had to have earned their status. Indeed, given the choice, Steve would have given his back teeth to become the most famous striker to have played for Grimsby Town.

Sport played a large part in his upbringing. He was raised in Cleethorpes, Lincolnshire where he was born 3 June 1968 to two schoolteachers, Marion and Paul Graham. He was a bright pupil at Haverhill Comprehensive School though he possessed a vein of insolence. In Year 11 he was suspended for a week for suggesting as the topic for a modern history research project an assessment of the number of people who died of natural causes at Auschwitz. Steve was a natural sportsman with a particularly aggressive nature on the football field even at times towards his own team members. He is said to have introduced sledging into the school's first cricket XI particularly with his habit of confiding to opposing batsmen while fielding in the slips that their mothers were part-time prostitutes. It was through sport that his journalism was both born and developed. His first stab at the art was for a write-up of a football match for the school magazine. He assessed his own team's players with hyperbole and as many long words he could muster to give a glowing account of the magnificent role each had played in the game. They'd lost 9-0!

After passing his A Levels with flying colours, in 1986 Steve attended Leeds University for a four-year degree in Sports Psychology. He became an enthusiastic member of the Socialist Society. His sporting activities were curtailed in the second year when he broke his leg after falling off the faculty roof after supplanting the university flag with that of the Republic of Cuba. In Steve's penultimate year he spent two terms studying at East Berlin's Dynamo Sports Academy. It was to have a lasting effect on him in several ways. He fell in love with an East German athlete, Britta Schopenhauer, and as his secondment neared its end he applied for an exit visa so that she could join him in Britain. The Ministry for State Security, the STASI, saw an opportunity for blackmail by suggesting it would grant the visa in exchange for Steve's supplying information on a certain university academic. Indeed, Steve complied by sending intelligence, albeit of low-grade, to his East German masters, in so doing betraying a fellow member of his college but, above all, betraying himself. Before long though, the romance ended, so too the need for the visa and the spying.

After Berlin, Steve found religion and left the Socialist Society. It's probable that there was a connection. He'd witnessed at first hand a Godless repressive Marxist-Leninist application at work. With his uncompromising approach to life, he rejected the Church of England's approach to religion in which he was nominally brought up as being "one that scarcely required belief". Instead, he embraced Catholicism that he considered "holier". In 1992 he married Maria di Angeli whom he met a church function. By now he had established himself as a sports writer on the Cleethorpes Chronicle, first as a reporter and subsequently as sports editor. His elegant turn of phrase and his opinions on local, national and even international sporting matters eventually brought him to the attention of the national media and in 2001 he ventured south to work for The National Herald. His profile rose after he had suggested that a certain Chelsea midfielder with a penchant for spectacular dives should don ballet shoes and a tutu rather than a football strip. This prompted the said player to do exactly that for a Football Focus interview the following Saturday. Despite many successful years, he eventually found that writing about sport, particularly the increasingly negative dimensions of the commercialisation of it, was starting to affect his enjoyment. Having listened to my waffling on the subject of obituaries that I produced for BBC News on many a train journey we shared, he applied and was accepted for the role of obituary writer on the Herald that he continued with distinction for more than two and a half years until his untimely death.

As so often with individuals who embrace ideas and institutions with an almost obsessive passion, they can drop them with equal measure. Gradually Steve rejected the dualist religious notion of a body and soul in favour of the physicalist idea of the human as an amazing yet solely material object. Swept up in the so-called New Atheism of the early 21st century, he found himself at odds with friends and family but remained steadfastly implacable. His constant search for truth was played out too on a smaller scale in the obituaries he wrote. If he stumbled upon family secrets his default inclination was to publish them since he firmly believed the dead deserved the truth. He never sought out such details in a manner of a sleazy tabloid hack, but if they were volunteered in answer to searching questions he would invariably lap them up. His conviction that obituaries were written for the benefit of the Herald's readers and not for the family was often mistaken by friends of the deceased for callousness. Yet behind the search for truth and the mordant wit was a man capable of great kindness. When a Herald colleague, a single mother, fell ill, he and Maria took in her six-year-old daughter for a week, driving her the eight-mile journey to school and back each day. Similarly, he once cycled 20 miles to visit a junior sub-editor who had become ill with depression.

Yet there was a certain paradox between the man who wished to expose the truth behind people's lives and the man who could be impenetrable or nebulous when it came to divulging matters within his own life. Nevertheless he remained a person of great fun and vitality who was never afraid of controversy and who railed against injustice of whatever magnitude. He was a fine journalist and a generous admirer of other people's work too as his daily tweets and retweets attested. His legacy will be that he gave a posthumous voice to the lives of so many ordinary folk from whom one can learn so much about one's own life.

Steve Graham, obituary writer, is survived by his wife Maria and his two children Naomi and William.

27 POST SCRIPT

Following the funeral at St Ignatius Catholic Church, Maria having decided it would be the full Catholic Mass since for once Steve was in no position to object, Ben, Robbie and Hilary caught the train home. They spoke of the excellent attendance. When Ben approached two young girls who clearly knew no one else at the gathering they turned out to be Gloria and Doreen from Espresso Bongo. Darren Simmons, quite recovered from his recent heart attack, had delivered the eulogy. Britta had not attended having returned to Germany while a forlorn looking Naomi and William had placed a floral panda on their father's coffin. The police had meanwhile raided the home of Aga Demir and caught him trying to escape through the back garden. They discovered a rucksack containing what forensic examination confirmed as dried deposits of Steve's blood. He confessed to the murder describing it as an "honour killing". According to Demir, Steve had insulted both his family and Islam by asserting that his grandfather was a homosexual despite the cottaging conviction that Demir described as being trumped up. Inwardly, Ben was furious that such a needless inclusion of the Demir name in Gunter's obituary had cost Steve his life. His obsession with the truth and for superfluous details had done for him. The Ogre was on duty and asked to see their tickets. He nodded his approval on inspecting them and before he turned to leave, he offered his condolences to Ben on the loss of his friend. Taken aback, Ben could only nod and offer a mumbled thank you. The three of them looked at each other in amazement and as The Ogre left the carriage they burst out laughing. As Hilary said, "People never fail to surprise you."

Acknowledgements

Thanks to Chris, Andy, Caroline and Debbie for their unwitting influence, to Martin Ouvry for his insightful editing, to Nigel Starck for his inspirational Life After Death book, to Mike Collett for his encouragement and invaluable technical know-how, to Frazer and co for the design, to Kate and Dave for their promotional and creative support, to Jo and Jan for their enthusiasm and unstinting encouragement. Finally, to Ralphy who would sometimes curl up beside me on my desk and keep me company while I searched for inspiration.

3801620R00146

Printed in Great Britain
by Amazon.co.uk, Ltd.,
Marston Gate.